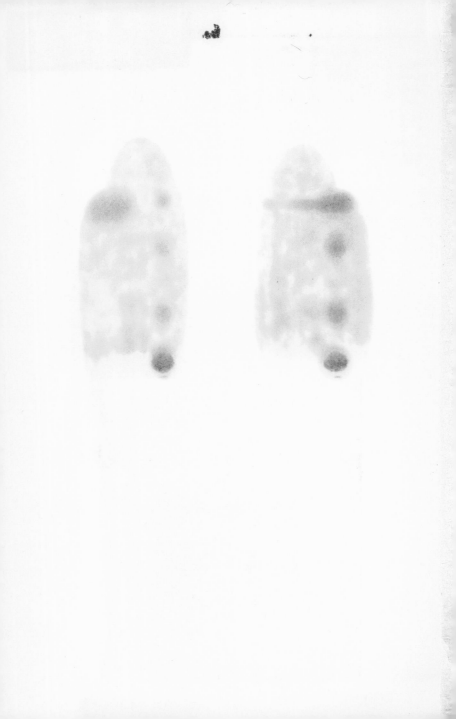

FIRE PATTERN

By the same author:

THE TWO-TIMERS
PALACE OF ETERNITY
ONE MILLION TOMORROWS
OTHER DAYS, OTHER EYES
TOMORROW LIES IN AMBUSH
ORBITSVILLE
NIGHT WALK
A WREATH OF STARS
COSMIC KALEIDOSCOPE
MEDUSA'S CHILDREN
WHO GOES HERE?
SHIP OF STRANGERS
VERTIGO
DAGGER OF THE MIND
THE CERES SOLUTION
A BETTER MANTRAP
ORBITSVILLE DEPARTURE

FIRE PATTERN

by

BOB SHAW

LONDON
VICTOR GOLLANCZ LTD
1984

First published in Great Britain 1984
by Victor Gollancz Ltd,
14 Henrietta Street, London WC2E 8QJ

British Library Cataloguing in Publication Data
Shaw, Bob
  Fire pattern.
  I. Title
  823′.914[F]   PR6069. H364
  ISBN 0-575-03452-1

sci fic

Set in Times by
A-Line Services, Saffron Walden
Printed in Great Britain by
St Edmundsbury Press, Bury St Edmunds, Suffolk

Prologue

"When you finally set yourself alight," Maeve Starzynski said, "don't come crying to me."

"Very funny," her father replied, vigorously brushing flecks of glowing tobacco from the front of his cardigan. He had been smoking his oldest briar, the one with the green insulating tape around the stem, when a sudden cough had sent ash spouting from the bowl.

"I'm not trying to be funny. Smoking is a disgusting habit. All the doctors say it's bad for your health."

"They're talking about cigarettes—the pipe is different." Art Starzynski smiled in his special infuriating way, lowering his eyelids to screen off any sign of opposition to his views. "The pipe is good for a man. People who smoke pipes live longer than people who don't smoke at all."

"Yeah—because they poison the rest of us off."

Her father's eyes were almost closed, Buddha-smug. "Coffee," he said pleasantly. "Nice and hot, nice and fresh, and I don't want instant."

"Oh, I wish you *would* burn to death," Maeve snapped, not hiding her exasperation as she strode out of the room and went through to the kitchen at the rear of the house. Her father was only sixty, but he assumed the attitudes and made the demands of somebody much older, seeming to revel in the infirmity which had overtaken him a month earlier.

Maeve was as quiet as possible when preparing the coffee and setting out two mugs—banging crockery around was too obvious a way of expressing resentment—and while the water was coming to the boil she stood at the window and breathed deeply, forcing herself to relax. The news from Doctor Pitman about her father's X-ray tests had been unexpectedly good, suggesting that his abdominal pains resulted from nothing more than some vague colic. His medication was bound to conquer the problem in a day or two, then she would be able to get back to her job and resume a normal life.

Keep thinking about that side of it, she told herself. *Be positive!*

While she was waiting for the coffee to finish percolating she became aware of a sweetly heavy smell of burning drifting into the kitchen. She guessed that her father was, as occasionally happened, experimenting with an exotic new brand of tobacco. She poured the coffee, set the two mugs on a tray and carried it towards the front room. The sweetish odour grew overpowering as she moved along the hall and now she could actually see a light blue haze in the air—a first intimation that something out of the ordinary might be taking place.

"Dad?" Maeve opened the door to the sitting room and gasped with shock as she saw that it was filled with blue smoke. Dropping the tray, she ran into the room, fully expecting to see an armchair on fire. She had heard how quickly some modern furniture could burn and also knew how vital it was to get people clear of the fumes without delay.

There was no sign of a blaze, nor could she see her father anywhere.

It was difficult to make out anything through the billowings of the curious light blue smoke, but it seemed to Maeve that there was a blackened area of flooring near the television set. She went towards it, gagging on the sickening sweet stench in the air, and her hands fluttered nervously to her mouth as she saw that what she had taken to be a black patch was actually a large hole burned clear through the vinyl and underlying boards. Several floor joists were exposed, their upper surfaces charred into curvatures, but—strangely—there was no active flame. In the floor cavity, supported by the ceiling of the utilities room below, was a mound of fine grey ash.

"Dad?" Maeve looked about her uncertainly, fearfully, and

6

her voice was barely audible. "Dad, what have you been . . .?"

At that instant her slippered foot touched a slightly yielding object on the floor. She glanced downwards—still an innocent, with thresholds of terror still to cross—and when she saw what was lying there she began to scream.

The object, easily recognizable by its signet ring, was her father's left hand.

Chapter 1

The *Whiteford Examiner* was much like any other small-town newspaper which had reached the year 1996 in a healthy condition.

It had survived the electronic revolution largely because it was impossible to take a television set out on the back porch, find in it enough small ads and local gossip to make a day's reading, and drape it over one's face when the summer heat and the drone of insects had finally induced sleep. The paper's headquarters were in a narrow four-storey building in the main street, sandwiched between a modern department store and an even more modern bank. Its owners, the Kruger family, were proud that the *Examiner* building was listed as having historical and architectural interest, and each day a stat of the front page of fifty years earlier was posted in a glazed box by the front entrance.

Ray Jerome usually liked the working environment of the reporters' room on the second floor. There was a feeling of vitality about it, a sense of being close to the living heart of the community, which helped to fill the gap at the centre of his own life. The loss of his wife through illness and of his engineering job through redundancy had almost broken him at one stage, but the newspaper work—a complete change of direction—had come along at the right time. He had taken to it with all the zeal of an intelligent, lonely, middle-aged man beginning a new life and, as often happens in such circumstances, had created problems both for himself and those around him.

The first difficulty of the new day arose when Hugh Cordwell, the young journalist at the adjoining desk, began to compose his report about a clash between two juvenile gangs in one of Whiteford's most troublesome districts. Cordwell brooded for a moment, began typing rapidly with two fingers, and on his VDU there appeared the heading: POLICE CALLED TO GANGLAND FLASHPOINT.

Jerome leaned sideways to get a better look at the screen. "You're not going to let that go through, are you?"

Cordwell stared at the words and then at Jerome. "What's wrong with it?"

"A flashpoint isn't a geographical location—it's a temperature."

"This isn't one of your fancy technical journals," Cordwell said, his china blue eyes showing the first hint of resentment. "Plain American is good enough around here."

"But how can the police be called to a temperature?" Jerome decided to go for absurdity. "It's like saying there was an incident on thirty degrees Celsius, at the corner of ten degrees Fahrenheit."

"Bull," Cordwell commented. "You've got more shit than a Christmas turkey."

"There's no need to be like that about it—I was only offering some friendly advice."

"Shove your advice!"

"Charming attitude," Jerome said in injured tones, looking around for backing. "You try to guide someone's faltering footsteps in the general direction of literacy, and all you get. . . ."

He allowed the sentence to trail off as his roving gaze encountered the slim, elegantly tailored figure of Anne Kruger, the *Examiner's* chief editor. She had paused on the way in to her office, apparently overhearing the exchange between Jerome and Cordwell. A slight lift of her head as she went through the doorway told Jerome she wanted to speak to him. He stood up, threaded his way through a cluster of desks and joined her in the spacious room which overlooked Mayflower Square.

10

Before speaking to him she took off her brocade jacket, put it on a hanger and smoothed down her white silk blouse—a series of actions which made it clear to Jerome's watchful eye that she was one of those women who appear, in defiance of time and biology, to reach their physical best at the age of forty. She had black hair, high cheekbones and a touch of hauteur which often led Jerome to picture her in Spanish-style riding clothes.

"Ray, what was going on out there?" she said, sitting down at her desk.

Jerome took off his steel-rimmed glasses and began to polish the already brilliant lenses. "Who's to know what goes on in the mind of a juvenile? I simply mentioned to Hugh that he had misused a word and he. . . ."

"That juvenile, as you call him, is a good reporter," Anne cut in. "He's quick to get hold of the facts and quick to get them into print."

Jerome recalled, belatedly, that Cordwell was in the same age group as the men in whose company Anne liked to go water-skiing and hang-gliding at week-ends. It had been undiplomatic to describe him as a child, but there was such a thing as sticking to one's guns.

"But what about the language?" he said. "Doesn't that come into it?"

"I've been over this with you before. Any slips in grammar or usage are picked up by the Leximat. Why do you think we installed it in the first place?"

The computer should be an adjunct to the human brain, not a replacement for it, Jerome replied inwardly, then decided there was such a thing as sticking to one's guns too long. "I promise not to bother Hugh again. He's only got a university degree in journalism—it isn't fair to expect him to know the meanings of words."

"Drop it, Ray."

"Sorry. Sorry." Jerome was about to leave the office when he noticed that Anne had not given her customary dismissive flick of the head. "Was there anything else?"

11

"Yes. You're always telling me how good you'd be as a science correspondent—so I'm going to give you the chance to prove it." Anne handed him a scrap of paper on which she had written an address in a residential swath on the town's south side. "Contact a woman called Maeve Starzynski. There was a fire at the house last week and her father got burned to death."

"I saw the. . . ." Jerome paused, gripped by an uneasy premonition. "What kind of a science story is that?"

"I've just been talking to a friend in the coroner's office and he tells me there were some very unusual aspects to this particular fire. It sounds to me like spontaneous human combustion."

"Oh, *no*!" Jerome gave a scornful laugh, deliberately making it as explosive as possible to signal the strength of his feelings. "Don't do this to me, Anne. Don't do it to the *paper*. In the last few months we've been up to here in phony spiritualists, UFO nuts, telepathic twins and characters who foresaw airliner crashes but kept their mouths shut till afterwards. We're going to lose all credibility with our readers ."

"There's a great deal of evidence. . . ."

"There's *no* evidence! None at all! People who babble on about astrology and thought photographs and spoon-bending and telekinesis and card-guessing don't even know what the word evidence means."

"If you call up our 'Unexplained' file you'll be able to find. . . ."

"Nothing that hasn't been explained."

"Do you mind letting me finish just one sentence?" Anne's face darkened with aristocratic anger and for a moment Jerome could almost see it framed by a flat black sombrero. "If you look in the file you'll find that people sometimes do burst into flames for no reason, and you'll also find that the details are quite odd."

"No doubt I will," Jerome said sarcastically. "The human body has a built-in fire extinguisher which is otherwise known as blood. Four or five litres of it. Those people who combusted

12

must have been a touch anaemic, or—better still—perhaps they had two strange punctures in their necks. . . ."

"If you would rather try earning your living as a comedian instead of reporting for this newspaper I'm sure I can arrange a quick release for you."

A hard brightness in Anne's eyes told Jerome she was in a dangerous mood and that he was not going to evade the unwelcome assignment. He clamped his lips and nodded as she gave her end-of-interview wave, a limp-fingered flick of the hand which might have been directed against a bothersome gnat. Ignoring the amused looks from the other journalists, he returned to his desk and pressed the REF key on terminal. He called up the "Unexplained" file and ran his gaze down the list of headings which appeared on the screen. The list was extensive, reflecting the editor's personal interest in the subject, but there was no mention of spontaneous human combustion.

Jerome's sudden flickering of hope was doused as he backtracked and found "Auto-incendiarism", a word to which he took a dislike on sight, classifying it as one of the pretentious labels which abound on the lunatic fringes of science. He stared at the screen in distaste, fingers hovering over the keys, experiencing a broody reluctance to involve himself any further with Anne Kruger's foibles.

"Did old Randy Kruger work you over?" The question came from Julie Thornback, a petite and doll-like blonde who, in spite of being less than half Jerome's age, had a couple more years experience in journalism and liked to give him advice as from an old hand.

"No. We were having a nice little chat."

Julie nodded in casual disbelief. "Don't let her wind you up, Ray. You'll never guess what she had the nerve to say to Hugh and I."

"Hugh and me," Jerome said, hoping the correction would be enough to show he did not want to be disturbed.

"What?"

"You should have said 'to Hugh and me'."

Julie's lips moved silently as she tried the phrase out. "It doesn't sound right."

Jerome sighed. "Look at it this way—if Hugh hadn't been there, if Anne had been talking to you alone, would you have said she was talking to 'I'?"

"No."

"That's your answer then. Excellent fellow though Hugh undoubtedly is, we don't change the rules of English simply because he appears on the scene."

Hugh Cordwell, who had been deep in his gang war report, raised his head. "Are you sniping at me again, professor?"

Before Jerome could reply Anne Kruger came out of her office, instantly detected the charge in the atmosphere and accused him with a luminous stare. He blanked his VDU screen, stood up and walked out of the room, suddenly deciding that any kind of outdoor assignment was preferable to being in a psychological autoclave. Why should he elevate his blood pressure over the fact that youngsters whose job was communication cared little for the tools of their trade? What was it to him if the chief editor of an influential paper enthusiastically promoted belief in the paranormal? It was ironic that the first and only woman to stir any feelings in him since the death of his wife had to be Anne Kruger—the least compatible and least attainable of all—but that too was something he had to accept. To do otherwise was to invite hypertension.

Wincing a little from the arthritis in his left knee, Jerome went down the stairs and out past the front office. In the street he blinked to adjust his eyes to the morning sunlight, then crossed to where his car was parked in the shade of the trees lining Mayflower Square. He opened the trunk, took out a detergent spray and some paper towels and spent a few minutes cleaning bird droppings from the car's paintwork. When it had been restored to a satisfactory condition he placed the towels in a litter bin, got into the car and edged it into the traffic flow.

The address he had been given was almost ten minutes away

and he used the time to listen for news of the Mercury expedition which had been slung out of Earth orbit a week earlier. The three-man ship, *Quicksilver*, was the first ever to have been designed, built and launched by a private corporation, and coverage of its progress was the sort of thing Jerome had had in mind when pressing for the post of science correspondent. All he got on the radio, however, were reports of the Argentine-Chile war and of the Philippines continuing with atmospheric H-bomb tests in defiance of the UN injunction. Vietnam and Western Malaysia, the countries suffering most from Philippine fall-out, were gathering a joint invasion force in spite of having been warned off by every major power which had an interest in that theatre.

The reminder that his personal problems were microscopic compared to those facing humanity in general gave Jerome the idea that he should adopt a more relaxed attitude in life. He knew exactly the kind of story Anne wanted—so all he had to do to squelch the matter was to write the one she did not want to see. It had to be cold, factual, rational and—above all else—dull. He switched off the radio and began checking street numbers. The address he wanted was in the SE twenties and it turned out to be a framed bungalow of medium size, elevated from the street by a neatly tiered rock garden. Its masses of red, white and blue alpines might have been planted with a patriotic theme in mind. The house itself, Jerome noticed, bore no external signs of fire.

He parked, got out of the car and was locking the door when it occurred to him that he had been too preoccupied with logical arguments to think about the human tragedy involved. A woman had lost her father in particularly disturbing circumstances only a few days earlier, and there was no telling how she would react to finding a newsman on her doorstep. Now that he considered the matter, he should have telephoned for an appointment and perhaps have saved himself a journey. Maeve Starzynski could be staying elsewhere with relatives, for all he knew. Half hoping that was the case,

Jerome went up the steep concrete steps. He was breathing heavily by the time he reached the front door and his knee felt as though the joint interfaces had been dusted with powdered glass. *Only fifty years on the clock*, he thought as he rang the doorbell, *and the damned machine is wearing out fast*.

The chimes were answered almost immediately by a youngish but tired-looking woman, and he knew at once she was the dead man's daughter. She was wearing a charcoal suit and her face was round and pleasant, giving the impression of a bookish intelligence which Jerome found appealing.

"Good morning," he said. "My name is Rayner Jerome and I'm a reporter with the *Examiner*. I hate to intrude at a time like this, but my editor asked me to call. . . ."

"It's all right," she said in a resigned monotone. "Come in."

"Thank you." Jerome followed her into the house, noting that though her hair and clothing were acceptably neat they did not have the precise control he instinctively associated with her character type. He guessed she was making her own way through purgatory, seeking no help from outsiders, and his natural sympathy became stronger. He had been along the same road. She led the way into a copper-glinting kitchen, picked up a carton of tea bags and gave him an enquiring glance. Jerome nodded gratefully.

"I wasn't sure if anybody would come out to see me," she said as she prepared two mugs of tea. "I don't know your editor personally, but a friend in the Pythian Sisters said she would speak to her on my behalf. I'm glad you were able to call."

"So am I," Jerome said, floundering a little as he realised a new complication had been added to the situation. The bereaved woman had views of her own which might or might not coincide with those of Anne Kruger, and which in any case constituted another editorial pressure on him. He began to feel impatience, an urge to have done with the sad affair as quickly as possible.

"People can be so silly, so vindictive," Maeve Starzynski

went on. "They're saying my father had so much alcohol in his system that he flared up like a torch . . . as if alcohol isn't converted into other substances in the body . . . as if you store it up inside you like a gas tank . . . That's just plain silly, isn't it?"

"Extremely." Jerome drank some tea and set the mug down. "May I see the room where you had the fire?"

"Through here." Maeve led the way along the central hall and turned left into a sitting room which Jerome had passed when coming in. It was a corner room, with windows on two adjoining sides, furnished for comfort rather than style with deep settees and home-made bookshelves. Orange throwrugs on a floor covering of café-au-lait vinyl added to the general brightness and cheerfulness of the place. The walls and ceiling were close to being immaculate and the air was fresh. Jerome, who was familiar with the acrid stench which lingers for weeks at the scene of a house fire, looked around with some puzzlement. The only discrepant feature was a square of hardboard which had been placed on the floor near an empty television stand.

"There has been remarkably little damage," he said tentatively. "Usually when a house catches fire there's a lot. . . ."

"The house *didn't* catch fire," Maeve interrupted. "It was my father who caught fire and burned away to nothing." Her gaze wavered for an instant. "Almost nothing."

Jerome indicated the piece of hardboard. "I know this must be distressing for you, but is that where you found the body?"

Maeve shook her head, her face stubborn. "There wasn't any body to find. This is what I can't make people *understand*. My father was turned into a heap of fine ash. Cigar ash, almost. It was in there." She stooped and slid the hardboard aside, revealing a roughly circular black-edged hole about a metre across. It was traversed by floor joists whose upper edges were badly charred, and at the bottom of the cavity were visible the laths and plaster forming the ceiling of a basement room.

17

Jerome studied the strangely circumscribed fire damage, noting that there was only slight blistering on the nearby skirting board, and his mind balked at what he was being asked to accept. The amount of heat needed to incinerate a human body to the extent Maeve Starzynski had described should have seared everything within a sizeable radius, should have started a serious blaze. He waited a few seconds then abruptly raised his head and scanned the woman's face. Her gaze locked with his, her eyes candid, intelligent and very troubled.

I respect this person, Jerome thought. *But where is she trying to take me?*

"Would you mind telling me exactly what happened?" he said, beginning to walk around the room and examine the rest of its contents.

"It has to be done," she replied steadily. "The first point is that my father was smoking his pipe when I last saw him, and he had just gotten some hot ash on his cardigan."

Jerome paused in his circuit of the room, feeling an immediate stirring interest.

"No," Maeve said, anticipating his question. "I only mention it because the men from the coroner's office made such a fuss about it. There wasn't nearly enough ash to set his clothes on fire. And even if there had been it wouldn't explain anything important, would it?"

"I see what you mean."

"Secondly, my very last words to my father were, 'I wish you would burn yourself to death'."

Jerome halted again, shocked, aware of the conversational focus making an uneasy slide from straight reportage into murkier regions. Refraining from comment, he stroked the cool curvature of a millefiori paperweight which was sitting on a bookshelf.

"The main reason I mention that," Maeve went on, "is that it happened and it's the sort of thing some women would be stupid enough to develop a neurosis over, but I'm going to

18

keep it up front and let the fresh air blow around it. We were having a tiff about his smoking. I'm quick-tempered and that's what I said and we both knew I didn't mean it."

"I'm sure your attitude is absolutely correct. What happened next?"

"I went into the kitchen to make us some coffee, and I was in there maybe ten minutes while it was perking." Maeve gave a rueful smile. "Any time Dad had to make the coffee himself he used instant, but when I was doing it for him it had to be percolated."

"I see." Jerome, in spite of his instinctive desire to stay aloof from personalities, was beginning to see the dead man as an individual in his own right. It would have been better if Art Starzynski could have remained Subject X, but the room where he had met his ghastly and inexplicable death insisted on his being accorded a human identity. Everywhere Jerome looked there were mute testimonials to Starzynski having been a man, not an insurance company statistic. There were several unremarkable fossils which derived significance solely from the fact that he had chosen to retain them; a seed catalogue; framed certificates for proficiency in first aid; a little heart-shaped cachou box; antique military field-glasses; tobacco cans; foreign coins. A real person had spent a good part of his life in this room and the evidence seemed to suggest that something very strange had brought that life to a close.

". . . making the coffee I began to notice a sweet burning smell," Maeve was saying. "Heavy and sickly it was, the way you imagine incense would be. When I came into the hall I noticed some light blue smoke and when I opened the door the room was full of it. I couldn't see anything at first, then I saw this hole in the floor by the television set. There were no flames. Just this hole in the floor and . . . and. . . ."

Jerome returned to the paperweight and stared into its vivid closed universe, shamed by his eagerness to hear what was coming next.

Maeve took a deep breath and when she spoke again her

voice was light and unconcerned, the voice of a stranger. "All that was left of my father was a heap of fine ash. I wouldn't even have known it was him. I would have thought he had gotten clean out of the room if it hadn't been for his left hand. That was the only part of him that didn't burn. It was lying on the floor, right beside the hole."

Jerome felt a cool prickling on his spine. In part it was due to the overt content of what he had just heard, but in the main it was a reaction to the changes which had taken place inside him. At some indefinable point in Maeve Starzynski's story he had begun to accept every word she said as true—and that meant there was something wrong with his own private picture of the universe. As a small child first learning arithmetic Jerome had been amazed at how perfectly the whole system of numbers *fitted*. No matter how many times he added or multiplied or carried out other manipulations there was never a stray quantity left over, and to his infant mind that had seemed too convenient to be true. He had spent hours of his free time performing tortuous calculations he had designed to trick the numerical system into revealing its secret flaw, the place where adult mathematicians had papered over a crack, and he had given up the quest with great reluctance. Now, unexpectedly, after all the years, he felt as though he had discovered the flaw, the hidden place where numbers refused to do what they were told. He looked closely at Maeve and saw that her face was pale and strained.

"I haven't finished my tea," he said. "The kitchen?"

Maeve nodded and they left the sitting room. In the kitchen she closed both hands around her mug of tea and took sip after sip from it, her eyes staring past Jerome into the yellow-turfed back garden. An electric clock on the wall made faint scraping sounds.

Jerome finished his own drink and set the mug down. "I have one more question, but if you'd prefer not to. . . ."

"It's all right. I'm all right."

"Where is the television set?"

"Oh, that! The police took it away for tests. One detective—I can't remember his name—must have asked me a dozen times if it was switched on when I went into the room." Maeve looked wanly amused. "He seemed quite upset when I insisted it wasn't."

"Electricity used to be the answer to everything."

"But not any more," Maeve said. "Not to this."

"No." Jerome had been striving without success for an explanation of what had happened to Art Starzynski, and now he could feel the bizarre mystery of it invading his mind like a stealthy army. It was a curious sensation, pleasurable and oddly familiar, then he realised that for a brief period, and for the first time since her death, Carla had been entirely displaced from his consciousness. And what had done it had been the intellectual challenge, the stimulation he had always felt when tackling some beguiling problem in applied or pure logic. For a moment he saw himself as the emotional equivalent of a vampire, feeding on the suffering of others, and had to repress a twinge of guilt. He gave Maeve Starzynski what he hoped was a reassuring smile.

"There is bound to be an explanation for what happened to your father," he said. "I'll do my best to find it."

Chapter 2

The morgue was a low redbrick building discreetly positioned in the grounds at the rear of Whiteford Holy Cross Hospital. There were no windows in the outside walls and the sole entrance was an unmarked steel door. It was the kind of building one tended not to see, which could go unnoticed and unremembered in any urban setting, but its appearance produced a cold queasiness in Jerome's stomach.

His first impulse on leaving the Starzynski house had been to return to the office and familiarize himself with the stored data on spontaneous human combustion, then he had rejected the idea for philosophical reasons. He would have been working with nothing more than words, other people's words, at a remove from the phenomenon he proposed to investigate—which was hardly in accord with the scientific method. Also, if he wanted to prove himself to Anne Kruger it would help if he displayed drive and initiative. His call to the hospital had won him an immediate appointment with a Doctor McGrath, and while driving across town in the crystalline New Hampshire sunlight he had been buoyantly satisfied with himself.

Now, however, as he approached the morgue on foot, it was borne home to him that he was generally disinclined to enter a place where corpses were stored. In particular, he did not wish to look closely at a charred human hand, and his reasons for ever wanting to do so seemed to have evaporated. Reflected brightness from the metal door was warm on his face as he paused and looked for a bellpush. A few seconds later, although no scanner was visible, the door was opened by a tall greying man with the harrowed look of someone who had once been very fat and now was thin. His shirt and trousers bunched at the waist, reinforcing the impression that he had lost weight. He had a long, deeply-lined face, and he regarded Jerome with a kind of gloomy candour.

"Come inside," he said. "It's cooler in here."

Jerome cleared his throat. "Doctor McGrath? I'm Rayner Jerome."

"I guessed that." A gleam of Karloffian humour appeared in McGrath's eyes. "We don't get many casual callers here."

"I dare say." Reassured by the doctor's expert use of the common touch, Jerome followed him into a short corridor and waited while he closed the outer door. The air in the building smelled fresh, untainted by chemicals.

"So you're a science correspondent," McGrath said as they walked to a small, harshly-lit office. "I didn't know the *Examiner* employed such an animal."

"Well, they don't really know it either. I'm trying to steer things in that direction."

"I see. Are you qualified?"

"Not scientifically," Jerome said, wishing the question would not keep recurring. "But I used to be in engineering and the disciplines haven't gone to waste."

McGrath's deep-set eyes glinted as he sat down at a desk. "That sounded slightly defensive."

"Did it?" For a moment Jerome was prepared to be offended by McGrath's perception and unusual directness, then he realized he was being offered a rare opportunity to bridge the chasm that separates human beings. "I suppose that's because I wasn't too well qualified as an engineer, either. I was a draughtsman in a general engineering outfit and I handled what we referred to as day jobs—jobs that were too small to make it worth while putting them into the computer. I could have them sketched and checked and into the workshop while a programmer was still adjusting the angle of his chair."

"What went wrong?"

23

"The old hands in the workshop retired and a computer took over their jobs—and it couldn't read my drawings."

McGrath nodded thoughtfully, indicating to Jerome that he should sit down. "And you didn't want to work on the computer."

"I was born with one of my own."

"Something tells me," McGrath said, with the hint of a smile, "that it was quite an experience for you to talk to Arthur Starzynski's daughter."

Jerome smiled back, glad of the change of subject, and took out his notebook and pen. "According to what Maeve Starzynski told me, her father's remains looked as though they had been cremated. Is that correct?"

"No."

Jerome was relieved and disappointed at the same time. "She seemed so. . . ."

"A crematorium oven couldn't produce anything like that result in just a few minutes," McGrath cut in. "This isn't the sort of thing people usually like to discuss, but I can tell you that when a cadaver is cremated it is subjected to 1,200 degrees Celsius for ninety minutes, and then to one thousand degrees for anything up to three more hours. Even then, what comes out of the oven is far from being fine ash or dust. You get a *lot* of bone fragments which have to be pulverized by machine, but in Starzynski's case there was only fine ash. Except for the hand, of course."

Jerome paused in his note-taking, aware that his jaw had almost sagged while he was absorbing the figures just quoted. McGrath stared back at him in morose satisfaction, his face like hewn marble in the sterile glow from the tubes in the ceiling. From another part of the building there came the faint rumble of a sliding door, sounding like distant thunder.

"That makes it all the harder to accept," Jerome finally said, wishing he could have produced a less obvious comment. "What sort of temperature would have been needed?"

"I don't know—interesting field of experiment there—but

24

the small change in Starzynski's pants pocket was fused into a single lump."

"May I see it?"

"The police took that and it's my guess they sent it up to Concord for forensic examination." McGrath stood up, took an overlong jacket from the back of his chair and shrugged it on. "Come and have a look at the *real* evidence."

Jerome got to his feet, experiencing a sudden timidity, and closed his notebook. "Is it pretty gruesome?"

"Good God, no." McGrath emitted a dry laugh. "A dish of chicken livers is ten times more unattractive than this little lot. I don't know how my wife can bring herself to make paté." As he was leading the way out of the office and along the corridor he glanced down at Jerome's notepad. "You must be the only reporter in the country who still writes shorthand."

"I've always used it, even when I was doing part-time work with a trade journal."

"Part of your one-man boycott of the electronics industry?" McGrath paused at a double door. "What's wrong with a recorder?"

"A recorder is fine for dictation. It can even cope, after a fashion, with a multiple conversation—provided everybody is obliging enough to speak in turn and you keep telling it who they are. But when you get a bunch of people arguing and mumbling and talking over each other and using gestures and facial expressions to carry their meaning a good shorthand note is far superior."

"And are you good at it?"

"Nearing three hundred words a minute."

"I might have guessed," McGrath said with an enigmatic expression. He opened the door and they went into a large room, clinically white, which had triple rows of square doors built into two walls. Jerome was surprised to hear bluegrass music, then he saw a chubby young man who was sitting at a desk and listening to a pocket radio while he ate pink-filled

25

sandwiches. The air was noticeably cold, causing Jerome to give a single shiver as it touched his skin.

"Don't be daunted by all this." McGrath made a sweeping gesture which took in the serried doors. "They're nearly all empty. The architect who designed the place must have thought we were a branch of CryoCare."

Jerome hunched his shoulders. "It certainly feels that way."

"Not another hothouse plant!' McGrath went to the desk and rapped it imperiously with his knuckles before speaking to the plump youngster. "Forgive me for interrupting your dedicated pursuit of obesity, Mervyn, but we want to view the Starzynski remains."

"Number eight," Mervyn said, handing him a set of keys.

"Thank you." McGrath switched off the radio, drawing a startled glance from its owner, beckoned to Jerome and went to one of the lockers.

He opened the door and pulled at a drawer which rolled out easily on telescopic cantilevers. Wisps of vapour drifted down its sides. Jerome moved closer on reluctant legs and saw that the drawer held two plastic bags. One was full of grey-black ash and the other, already dewing over with condensation, contained Art Starzynski's left hand. The wrist tapered to a black point and the fingers were straight and splayed out, as though Starzynski had experienced an electrifying pang of astonishment or terror in the instant before he was overtaken by death.

Jerome stared down at the grotesque object, prepared for revulsion, but found in himself a curious lack of emotion. The destruction and dehumanization of Art Starzynski had been too complete. The hand could have been a relic of Ancient Egypt, or a fossil, too divorced from the immediacy of life to have any significance for those who still breathed and could feel the warm cardiac tide in their veins.

"See what I mean about the consistency of the ash?" McGrath said, gently prodding the larger bag with one finger. "I just don't know what temperature it took to do this. A *lot* of heat was involved."

26

"But there was practically no fire damage in the rest of the room."

"So they say." McGrath gave a dismissive shrug. "I'm glad I don't have to establish the root cause of what happened to this man."

"Have you no theories at all?"

"The only one I would have given any credence to is that Maeve Starzynski either killed her father or found him dead, then dismembered him and spent a week or so reducing the pieces in a high-powered furnace."

Jerome sniffed to signal his scepticism. "Why should she do that?"

"I've no idea—my only concern is with explaining the physical condition of the remains—but the theory is useless anyway, because neighbours were talking to Starzynski less than an hour before he died. Are you through in here? Are the eyes sufficiently feasted?"

"Yes, and I think I understand the problem better now. Thanks for giving me your time."

"Glad to be of service." McGrath slid the drawer and its macabre contents back into the wall, locked the door and returned the keys to the young man at the desk. Mervyn nodded silently, beginning to unwrap another sandwich, and before McGrath and Jerome had fully left the room it was again pervaded by the incongruous strains of bluegrass.

"Some people," McGrath commented sadly, "have no respect for the dead."

It was a little past noon when Jerome got back to the *Examiner* building. Most of the ten desks in the reporters' room were occupied, but the noise level was low and the atmosphere was relaxed. The midday lull signified that all the major deadlines for that evening's paper had been successfully met, that human brains could coast until quitting time while machine intelligences took over the job of getting the paper on to the streets. It was a period Jerome savoured for two reasons. As a latecomer to the profession, he felt it linked him to the historic days of journalism when stout shoes were an essential, the work could be physically demanding and there was a glow of personal achievement each time a paper was put to bed. Also, he liked the freedom from noise and interruptions which enabled him to make good progress with his work.

He collected a cup of iced tea from the dispenser, went straight to his own desk and sat down, swearing under his breath as his left knee produced a defiant stab of pain. The tea was cloyed with artificial sweetener, but cold enough to be refreshing. He opened his notebook and began to study his record of the morning's two interviews, glad of the opportunity to think calmly about what he had learned. A few seconds later he became aware of somebody standing at his side. He looked up and saw Hugh Cordwell, who was in a jovial mood now that the pressure of work had eased, peering over his shoulder at the pages of shorthand.

"Squiggle, squiggle," Cordwell said. "Squiggle, dot, squiggle."

"That's the most perceptive remark you've made in ages," Jerome said. "What do you want, Hugh?"

"Randy Kruger is mad at you."

"Why?"

"You'll find out the reason why soon enough."

"'The reason why' is a tautology," Jerome pointed out, hoping to detract from the younger man's evident pleasure. "And your utterances never merit repetition."

A reporter at a nearby desk snorted in amusement, causing Cordwell's eyes to shuttle angrily as he sought a reply. "Squiggle, squiggle," he said finally, before returning to his seat.

"The spirit of the Algonquin lives on," Jerome muttered. He tried to think of something he had done to earn Anne Kruger's displeasure, but his mind was quickly drawn back to the infinitely greater problem represented by a human hand and a mound of ash. A man called Art Starzynski had died a strange and terrifying death, and nobody could explain why. Or could they? Jerome found that he now had an intense interest in the *Examiner's* file on auto-incendiarism—if other people had died in similar circumstances the phenomenon was bound to have been investigated and the findings put on record.

Setting his tea aside, he activated his desk terminal and called up the related index pages, aiming to get a broad impression of the extent of the file. He had been prepared for a chronology going back a decade or two, and so it was with a distinct sense of shock that he picked out a listing of the year 1852 coupled with the name of Charles Dickens. More intrigued than ever, he screened further details and learned that Dickens had disposed of one character in *Bleak House*— Krook the money-lender—by having him undergo spontaneous incineration while alone in his room. Frowning, aware of an uncomfortable speeding up of his heart, he raced through an extract from the novel, his gaze skipping from phrase to key phrase . . .

The cat has retreated . . . and stands snarling . . . at something on the ground, before the fire . . . smouldering suffocating vapour in the room . . . small burnt patch of flooring . . . and here is—is it the cinder of a small charred and broken log of wood sprinkled with white ashes, or is it coal? O Horror, he IS here! and this from which we run away, striking out the light and overturning one another into the street, is all that represents him.

Jerome sat back and stared at the glowing words on his VDU, wondering where the dividing line between fact and fiction actually lay. He had always thought of Dickens as a chronicler of the social conditions of his day, not as a reporter of phenomena in the dark hinterland of science. The description of what had happened to Krook, apart from one reference to contamination of the ceiling, so closely paralleled the fate of

Art Starzynski as to make it clear that Dickens was no stranger to the notion of spontaneous human combustion. Another fact which Jerome found striking for a different kind of reason was that he had read *Bleak House* at least twice in his youth, but had retained no memory of such an unusual episode. It was as though a highly conservative and sceptical censor in his mind had decreed against the storage of obvious heresies.

Having broached the subject of classic literary references to the fire death, Jerome went further on and was fascinated by the discovery that it had been touched upon by such writers as Mark Twain, Washington Irving, Balzac, Marryat, de Quincey and Zola. Several of the books mentioned were familiar to Jerome but, again, the relevant passages were gone from his memory. Marryat was among those who went into detail, in a novel entitled *Jacob Faithful* published in 1834, emphasizing the point that although the victim had died in her sleep— completely reduced to black ash—the curtains of the bed had not even been singed.

But that's impossible, was Jerome's instinctive protest; then he recalled the curious localization of the fire damage in the Starzynski house—paintwork only a single pace away from the site of combustion had not even discoloured. Feeling baffled, almost personally affronted by the screaming scientific anomaly, he took off his glasses—transforming his surroundings into a complex blur—and polished the lenses, something he did almost unconsciously when he needed time to think. It was difficult enough to accept that a sponge filled with salty water, which was how one might regard a human body, could spontaneously generate furnace-core heat, but to go a giant step further and envisage that awesome heat being contained. . . .

"*There* you are!" Anne Kruger had appeared at his side as if by magic. "How was your vacation, Ray?"

Recognizing that she needed to vent some angry sarcasm, he gave the reply she wanted. "I haven't been on vacation."

"Really! I was under the impression that you had."

Brilliant witticism, Anne, he thought, replacing his glasses and bringing her face into sharp focus. "Does this mean I've forgotten to do something?"

There was a white beacon-flash from her eyes. "Ray, I've just looked through the make-up of today's paper and I didn't see your fire story in it."

"My fire st—!" Jerome was shocked and indignant. "You can't expect a piece like that to be written in a couple of hours."

"That's true—I'd have said something in the region of ten minutes."

"Anne, this isn't one of your fry pan fires—four lines on page twenty—there's an important story here. It looks as though a citizen of this town simply burst into flames and burned away to almost nothing."

"I'm the one who mentioned SHC to you in the first place. Remember? You as good as said I was crazy."

"I know, and I'm sorry about that," Jerome said, genuinely apologetic, aware of Cordwell grinning at him from the neighbouring desk. "I prejudged the matter without looking at the evidence, but I've just come back from the morgue and what I saw there. . . ."

"You went and actually looked at the body?"

"Remains is a better word."

"I didn't realize you'd gone that far into it." Anne's voice had become more amiable. "All right, come into the office and we'll have a talk."

"Gladly." Jerome stood up and nodded pleasantly to Cordwell, who promptly turned away. As he followed Anne to her office, breathing an invisible wake of French perfume, Jerome was again impressed by her physical attractiveness. Only ten years separated them, yet she managed to personify freshness and vitality, whereas he seemed to have been precipitated from youth into middle age with no noticeable interval between. Perhaps, if he had persevered more with contact lenses—as Carla had always urged—and had kept himself in

31

trim, and had learned to dress younger, and had acquired more money. . . . The list, he suddenly realized, could grow for ever, and its compilation was an exercise in futility.

In her office Anne questioned him closely about Maeve Starzynski's reliability as a witness and about the circumstances surrounding the bizarre death. Jerome passed on what information he had, giving due prominence to the inexplicable features of the case.

"This could do the paper a lot of good," she said when he had finished. "We seem to have this one to ourselves and there's a good chance of getting it syndicated. I'm going to give you the rest of today and tomorrow to write a good strong feature, with that by-line you've been plaguing me for. Get some good pictures, especially of the hand, and tie Starzynski in with as many classic cases as you can . . . Doctor Bentley and so on . . . and we'll give the story a full page in Friday's paper. . . .

"What's the matter, Ray? You look as though you're sitting on your keys."

Jerome shifted unhappily. "I don't see how the article could be squeezed on to one page."

"Why not?"

"It's too big! You could use several pages just to examine possible causes, and then there's. . . ."

"You're not going to write a book," Anne snapped, then she gave him a patient smile. "There *isn't* a scientific explanation for SHC. That's the whole essence of it—it's a supernatural event."

"Do you realize what you just. . . .?" Jerome gave an exaggerated sigh. "Anne, there *has* to be an explanation. For every effect there has to be a cause."

"That's 19th century thinking. Modern scientists take a different view."

"I've never heard them say so. Name just one scientist who says that."

"Well, they're admitting there are things they can't explain."

32

"Yes, but admitting you haven't found an answer isn't the same as saying no answer exists."

"Tell me just one thing," Anne said, a tinge of pink appearing on her cheeks. "Has anybody come up with a scientific explanation for SHC?"

"Ah . . . not that I know of."

"And are you going to find an answer this afternoon?"

"I shouldn't think so."

"Then why in the name of God should you waste my time and your time and the time of our readers with useless speculation? Are you going to write this story properly, or would you prefer that I hand it over to Cordwell?"

"I'm going to write the story properly," Jerome said stiffly. "I appreciate the way you give a person scope for initiative in these things."

He stood up and left the office, retaining as much dignity as he could, and returned to his desk, marvelling at the speed with which he had managed to win his editor over and then freshly antagonize her. Disguising the fact that the interview had gone badly, he hummed some Gilbert and Sullivan as he began to work through the computer files. For a few minutes his concentration was marred by lingering resentment towards Anne Kruger, but the sounds of the big office gradually faded from his consciousness as he was drawn into his subject.

He was again surprised by the antiquity of some of the records. The first detailed example to which he had access had occurred in Rheims in 1725, and by 1763 a Frenchman, Jonas Dupont, had already gathered enough case histories to enable him to publish a book called *De Incendis Corporis Humani Spontaneis*—the first full account of the phenomenon. Jerome had anticipated vagueness and an apocryphal quality to the reports, but from the start it was as if witnesses—anticipating scepticism—had gone out of their way to be precise and positive. The dates, names and exact addresses were there and were easily verifiable, with very little of the "Mr Green of New Jersey" style of vague reporting which characterized most of

33

the dubious research work Jerome had seen published in other fields. Time after time, varied only by circumstantial detail, there unfolded the same tale of horror, inexplicable and frightening, threatening to undermine his belief in the essential rationality of the universe.

One aspect of SHC he found particularly disturbing was its sheer randomness. Other investigators appeared to have been troubled by the same thing, because the literature was permeated with their attempts to find a pattern, any kind of a link between victims. In the 18th and 19th centuries it was thought that a precondition for the fire death was an addiction to alcohol—not beer or wine, but hard liquor. Jerome could sympathize with the desire to attribute SHC to the heavy consumption of "ardent spirits", and it did seem to be a common factor in early cases, but he put that down to the fact that the vast majority of ordinary people in those times drank to relieve the miseries of existence. As the chronology advanced close to the present more and more instances were recorded of moderate drinkers and abstainers meeting the same gruesome death.

With his computerized overview of the centuries, Jerome saw other candidates for the elusive common factor come into favour and win acceptance, only to be ground down again by the mill of statistics. At one stage the preferential victim would tend to be an elderly female, or greatly obese, or a pipe smoker—but the accumulation of case histories eventually ironed out every peak in every graph. One factor in which Jerome took an intuitive interest was that the victims were of solitary habits, or had at least lived alone, but that too had to be discarded. There were many examples of men, women and even children suddenly bursting into flames while surrounded by others and within minutes being reduced to ash. It had happened in dance halls, in boats and cars, in sports stadiums. In Chicago in 1982, and again in Montreal in 1994—to select but two examples—people had spontaneously combusted and died while walking in busy streets.

34

At frequent intervals during the work Jerome experienced a reaction, a kind of personal rebellion against the nature of his subject matter. *This just can't be true*, he would think. *Somebody with a sick imagination invented this stuff.*

But the pictures were there to prove him wrong.

The pictures were there in disturbing high resolution—a sickening parade, photographed with a clarity which simultaneously repelled the eye and seduced it into searching for fresh horrors. There was also a bludgeoning similarity to the images. Jerome became numbed by the heaps of white-flecked ash whose only discernible connection with humanity were the appendages, here a slippered foot, there a hand lying like a discarded glove.

By the time he had skimmed every page stored in the *Examiner*'s library he had satisfied himself of only one thing—the sole pattern was the complete lack of pattern. He was being asked to accept that *anybody* might suddenly be consumed by fire at any place and at any time. The evidence suggested that it was a purely random event, uninfluenced by anything in the victim's circumstances or physical condition—and Jerome found the notion totally repugnant.

His thesis was that there had to be a logical explanation for SHC, no matter how deeply buried. But underlying rationality was supposed to reveal itself to the enquiring mind sooner or later. In the case of such a startling and well-documented phenomenon as SHC it should have been easy to detect a pattern or pinpoint a common factor, but that was precisely what had not happened. Many minds had grappled with the problem for many decades; the "explanations" put forward ranged from divine retribution to poltergeists to new classes of sub-atomic particles; and nowhere was there even the beginning of an indication of why one person rather than another should be singled out to become a human torch. To make matters worse in Jerome's eyes, the various theorists—some of whom had written massive books on the subject—had fallen at the preliminary hurdles. The curious localization of

35

the heat was a classic feature of SHC, one which had excited wonder and comment down the centuries, and nobody had advanced anything resembling a reason . . .

"The job doesn't pay overtime, you know." Anne Kruger spoke from the doorway of her office, startling Jerome. He looked about him and saw that it was past seven in the evening. He had been distantly aware of the other reporters locking their desks and going home, but he had not noticed being on his own for three hours. His eyes were smarting from the protracted sessions with the VDU and there was an ominous pain in his lower back which suggested he had made himself overtired.

"I guess I got absorbed," he said. "There's no harm in knowing the background."

"Don't be defensive, Ray—I approve of my staff being thorough." Anne came towards him, vivid and gleaming, freshly made up for going out, and he felt a pang of jealousy towards some unknown youngster in tennis shorts. "How are you getting on with it?"

"I know practically everything there is to know about spontaneous human combustion."

"I'll bet you do—I'd give anything for a memory like yours." Her brown eyes were sympathetic. "Have you thought about stopping for a bite to eat?"

Jerome indulged a reckless impulse. "No. Where shall we go?"

"I know where *I'm* going," Anne replied, at once resuming the boss-employee relationship. "And I suggest that you eat something soon before you win yourself an ulcer."

"Yes, ma'am." He smiled, concealing his self-disgust over making the gaffe, and watched her walk to the elevator. She looked youthful, self-sufficient and confident, the sort of person who would have achieved success even if her father had not owned a newspaper. Jerome imagined himself as her partner for an idealized evening . . . the excellent food and wine . . . the dancing . . . the return to a plushy apartment

36

. . . the scented waxy taste of lipstick, which he was close to forgetting. . . .

Swearing at himself for having opened mental doors which were best left closed, he surveyed the office with tired eyes. The red-gold sunlight slanting in from the windows made the desks and equipment seem irrelevant to anything, artifacts which people had long ago put into storage when they had gone off to attend to the real business of life. This was no place for him to be on a fine August evening, but what was the alternative? His home on the north side would be just as lonely, the more so because Carla had loved this time of year, and it was too late to consider driving out to the old chalet at Parson's Lake.

Jerome took off his glasses and polished the lenses while he weighed the matter. He intended to keep on working until at least midnight, thus guaranteeing that sleep would come easily, and the research could be done almost as efficiently at home. The main difference, he decided abruptly, was that at home he could sit in a more comfortable chair and ease the tiredness in his lower back. And his own tea was marginally better than what came out of the office machine.

That's it, he thought, gathering up his notebook and pencils. *There's nothing like having clearly defined goals in life.*

A few minutes of bathing his eyes had such a soothing effect that he decided he could watch television for a short while before resuming work. He cleared away the remains of the Waldorf salad he had picked up at Harpo's on the way home, and eased himself into his best armchair, carefully balancing a glass of iced tea. When he remotely activated the television set, the news channel he usually watched was preoccupied with the Argentine-Chile conflict and the breakdown of the chemical warfare talks in Paris.

Jerome, who had been seeking information about the Mercury shot, listened to the reports with growing unease. He had been born the year after World War II had ended, and

37

had grown up through various phases of the Cold War with an instinctive belief in the race's ability to muddle through any crisis. As was the case with most ordinary citizens, sheer practice had made him adept at preserving his natural optimism, at disregarding the prophets of doom, but lately he had begun to feel afraid. It might have been a psychological reaction to the death of his wife, but now it seemed entirely possible to him that the politicians and generals were on the verge of ending *all* human life.

Jerome had a theory that it was the prospect of racial extinction which on a subconscious level was fuelling the public's interest in the *Quicksilver's* mission to Mercury. Until the previous year the arid little planet, so uncomfortably close to the sun, had been a low-priority target for any kind of mission, let alone one carrying three men. Then a space-borne telescope had picked up a curious reflection. Studies of the enhanced images suggested that they showed a bus-sized area of highly machined metal lying on the surface of Mercury at the northern pole.

As soon as all members of the space club had denied knowledge of the object the speculations about a contact from Outside had begun, and within days there was a widespread semi-religious belief that an interstellar ship had landed or crashed on Mercury. At one end of the credulity spectrum this was proof that help was on the way, that a benign intervention was going to save humanity from itself; at the other, it was the thin consolation of knowing that Man had at least been noticed and his self-immolation would be an object lesson for others. Either way, the mysterious object lying on the pitted surface of Mercury represented a stake in eternity, and public interest in a space flight was higher than at any time since the first lunar landings.

Tiring of the news broadcast, Jerome switched over to computer mode, keyed in to the *Examiner's* central processor and began a more careful reading of the pages which had suggested causes for SHC. He found portentous references to involuntary reorganization of muscle cells which changed people into million-volt batteries, to Elijah and the divine fire, to *botulinus*-poisoning patients developing bioluminescence, to neutron weapons, to da Vinci's belief that the chief function of the heart was to develop heat, to the Earth's magnetic field, to incendiary ghosts, to undetected atomic particles called pyrotons . . .

In Jerome's opinion the wordage was nothing more than semantic floundering, and a two-hour exposure to it confirmed his original view that nobody had ever come near a reasonable explanation for the fire death. He tried a different approach and looked for statements on the subject by qualified scientists, only to find that all those listed flatly denied the existence of the phenomenon. He was not too disappointed, remembering that he had been equally dogmatic about it only twelve hours earlier, but at the same time it would have been useful from the point of view of the article to have some kind of authoritative comment. Get plenty of quotes, Anne was always urging him, apparently in the belief that a reporter's unsupported word did not carry much weight. He considered the problem for a moment, then remembered having been impressed by the sound thinking and dry humour of one writer, John Sladek, who in 1994 had published a no-nonsense study of the paranormal in a book called *Psychic Superstars*.

Jerome had consulted the work in the afternoon and had found no references to SHC, but that did not necessarily mean that Sladek had no thoughts on the subject. On the spur of the moment Jerome used the computer to get an address and phone number for Sladek, and discovered he was living in New York. Without hesitating, in case he lost momentum, he picked up the extension phone from beside his chair and put a call through. It was answered immediately.

"I'm sorry about disturbing you after hours, Mr Sladek," Jerome began. "My name is Rayner Jerome, and. . . ."

"You're not a bill collector, are you?" Sladek cut in.

39

"No. I'm a reporter with the *Whiteford Examiner*, and I'd like to ask your help on a story because I was very much impressed by your book on the paranormal."

"Thank you. It's nice to hear from one of my readers . . . Wonder who the other one is?"

Jerome gave an obliging chuckle. "It's about this weird business of spontaneous human combustion. I noticed you didn't touch on it in the book, and I was wondering if you believe in it or not."

"Oh, I don't know," Sladek said. "Maybe people do burst and make ashes of themselves."

"This is a serious enquiry," Jerome said, beginning to be annoyed by the other man's flippancy. "Have you any thoughts about SHC?"

"Well, it's a whole new category of event that the insurance companies can refuse to pay off for."

Jerome gave a sigh, making sure it was audible on the phone. "Thanks for your help, Mr Sladek—I'll leave you to get on with whatever you were doing in peace."

"No trouble at all, Mr Jerome," came the reply. "I'm sorry I couldn't tell you that spontaneous human combustion is done with mirrors."

Jerome slammed the phone down, resolving to have no further dealings with writers, and sat frowning at the wall opposite. Aware that he was in danger of becoming obsessive, that it would be much more advisable to relax with a glass of wine before going to bed, he shelved the idea of trying to link SHC victims prior to their deaths. There had to be a common factor—of that he was convinced—but it had either been missed out of the data or concealed by irrelevancies. He took his notepad and wrote down the similarities which became evident *after* the subjects had met their bizarre deaths. The list was short, containing only three items:

1. Little damage is ever done to nearby combustible materials, even when they are very close to the body. Quite often

40

the victim's clothes or bedding are untouched, although a temperature of at least 3,000° must have been generated in the body. (This, above all else, sticks in my intellectual craw.)

2. There is almost total consumption of the torso, and yet—for no known reason—some of the extremities often escape serious burning. If combustion is triggered by some physical condition, why should hands and feet be spared?

3. There is quite often an absence of smell—quite incredible when one considers what has happened—or there are references to a sweet smell. (Starzynski is a perfect example.)

Jerome stared down at his words, baffled by their content, tantalized by the idea that the key to the mystery of SHC might be there if only he could see it. He knew that a multitude of others before him had wrestled in vain with the same problem, many of them better equipped and prepared to devote years to their research, so it was—to say the least—highly presumptuous of him to hope for a break-through after only one day's work. But there is a discreet egotism which drives quiet men of the breed who get to attach their names to new stars or theorems; and in the stillness of midnight it seemed possible to Jerome that he could achieve that shift of perception, the one accompanied by the pre-orgasmic sensation in brain and gut, which suddenly cleaves opaque problems into diamond transparencies.

This is risky, he thought. *I'm too tired to think properly, and if I let a fugue get going in my head there'll be lots of nightmares and very little sleep before morning.*

As he had expected, the warning was disregarded by that part of his mind which had never been able to relinquish its grip on a riddle. He spent an hour going back over his notes on the most significant case histories. At one point it crossed his mind that there seemed to be an unduly high representation of English-speaking countries, but he was able to dismiss the bias by putting it down to his working in the English language, plus

41

poor reporting from other parts of the world. When his eyes became too weary to focus properly on words he stubbornly resorted to screening series of photographs.

Exhaustion had set in and was making him more vulnerable, preventing him from distancing himself from the succession of crematorium images, and gradually he drifted into a grim and sleazy universe, remorselessly detailed, which was largely composed of organic cinders. Human feet which terminated in nothing more than charred stumps of shin were pathetic and ludicrous objects, but entirely appropriate to the Dali landscapes in which he was wandering. They loomed like grotesque castles on ashy plains which were littered with the residue of past lives—reading glasses, coins, nail files, cigarette lighters, shattered cups, scraps of food. It was not great works for which SHC victims were remembered, but the trivia which the camera seemed to seek out and gloat over.

At 2.30 Jerome finally accepted that there was to be no visitation of Truth, that he was to remain in the ranks of ordinary men, and he went to bed. He dozed off almost immediately but, as he had feared, there were nightmares in wait and he awoke after a few minutes in the full, depressing knowledge that he would have no real sleep for the rest of the night. Names and dates and places seethed in his thoughts, and when accidental rhymes occurred they were seized upon and made into repetitious chants. He tried to relax and at least benefit from the physical inactivity, but each time he closed his eyes he was again looking at the pictures. In the past he had been grateful for his eidetic memory, but now it was a dreadful liability, causing him to flinch and squirm under the bombardment of images.

Perhaps an hour had dragged by when, unaccountably, one of the photographs steadied in his mind's eye. In his trancelike state he was able to recall at once that it showed the remains of Betty Ramon, an elderly widow who in 1989 had burned to death in her apartment in Great Falls, Montana. The picture had all the standard elements, from the flame-severed feet in

42

worn slippers to the black-rimmed hole in timber flooring. It was an unremarkable example of its kind, no more horrific in its sordid detail than a hundred others, and yet Jerome felt a strange sense of imminence which jolted him into alertness.

He sat up in the dark, wondering if he was the victim of a night-fevered mental prank, then decided he had nothing to lose by going back to the computer. When he got up and switched on lights the house and its furnishings had the slightly alien quality which is familiar to insomniacs, as though tenure belonged to others in the small hours and his waking presence at that time was an intrusion. He limped into the living room, perched uncomfortably on the front of his armchair and called up the Betty Ramon picture on his television screen.

The image, with its thousand-line definition, was so clear that he might have been looking through a window into a brightly-lit room. He studied it for a moment, baffled by the pounding of his heart, then his gaze was drawn to a single detail in the lower left-hand corner. There, camouflaged by the rosebud pattern of a bedroom carpet, was a tiny heart-shaped box. He stared at the object, realizing he must have subconsciously noted it during an earlier viewing, totally at a loss to explain his growing excitement. But something was happening in his head . . . neural switches were being thrown . . . memories were stirring. . . .

He had seen a similar box that very morning in the room where Art Starzynski had died.

"So what?" he said aloud, further expressing disappointment by turning off the computer with unnecessary force. Muttering in self-disgust, he went into the kitchen, poured a glass of cold milk and sipped it while he analysed what had happened. He knew from past experience that in the condition between wakefulness and sleep the mind's internal censor could cease to function. With the self-critical faculty lulled, the tritest idea could come as a world-shaking revelation. In this case his subconscious had got itself into a ferment by making a number of free-wheeling associations . . . cachou box . . .

pillbox . . . medication . . . side effects . . . alteration in body chemistry . . . common factor in spontaneous human combustion . . .

Nearly gave myself a heart attack over nothing, he thought as he rinsed his glass and dried it. He polished it with a soft cloth until long after it was dry, then he went reluctantly to bed.

Chapter 3

In the morning he got to within two blocks of the office before accepting that it was quite impossible for him to go in. Appalled by his own irrationality, he made a right turn at the next set of lights and aimed the car south. Whiteford was ablaze with sunlit familiarity, glowing with that aura of humdrum comfort, security and sanity which is special to small towns on summer mornings. People were abroad early, getting business done before the day's heat set in. Jerome knew that in the reporters' room at the *Examiner* the daily routine would be well under way, with Anne Kruger and her Castilian eyes absorbing every detail, especially the yawning emptiness at his desk. And what reason could he give her for his absence?

Well . . . you see, Anne . . . there was this funny looking pillbox. . . .

Jerome squirmed with embarrassment as he visualized the editor's reaction, but he continued driving towards the Star-zynski house. The notion that SHC victims were linked by a medicine which radically affected their metabolisms was far-fetched on its own, and it was compounded in lunacy by the idea that in a matter of hours he could have hit on a truth which had eluded other investigators for centuries. But it was lodged in his mind like a fish-hook, and the only way to free himself from the obsession was to check it out—even if he had to make a fool of himself in the process.

And that's exactly what I'm doing, he thought as he pulled up outside the neat house atop its buttresses of blossom and stone. He sat for a moment as he tried to dissociate himself from the venture and then, feeling hag-ridden, got out of the car. The concrete steps seemed more steep than before and he

45

was breathing noisily as he thumbed the doorbell. There was a delay of perhaps a minute before Maeve Starzynski appeared. She was wearing a flowered housecoat and her round face bore the uncertain expression of one who has just emerged from a long sleep.

"Oh," she said. And then, anticipating his apology, "No, it's all right—please come in."

"Thank you." Jerome went in and waited in the hall while she closed the door. More than a year of being a widower had heightened his sensitivity to such things, and in close proximity to the woman he found he could actually detect the smell of sleep from her. It was an evocative blend of warm bed linen, facial cream and light clean perspiration which made him realize how much he hated living alone. For one thing, with Carla around there would have been no midnight vigils at the computer . . .

"I took a sleeping pill last night and I guess it must have been a good one," Maeve said. "I don't much care for anything like that, but my doctor advised it."

Jerome nodded sympathetically. "I'm sorry about just showing up on your doorstep—it's a habit I seem to be getting into—but . . . well . . . I need some extra information."

"What is it?"

"I was wondering. . . ." Jerome strove to overcome his embarrassment. "Can you tell me if your father was taking any medication?"

"Yes." She gave him a quizzical look, went into the kitchen and returned with a bubble-strip of yellow capsules. "Colophazine-D. I don't know what kind of drug this is, but my father was prescribed it for abdominal pains."

Jerome's discomfort increased. "That's not what I meant. Did your father use any pills that are packaged in a little heart-shaped box?"

Maeve smiled, openly incredulous. "From ye olde apothecary? Of course not."

"I know how ridiculous all this sounds and I promise to go

46

away and stop being a nuisance as soon as possible—but what did he keep in the box?"

"Which box?"

Jerome blinked at her. "The little violet one. I saw it on a shelf in there." He indicated the closed door of the sitting room.

"I don't remember seeing him with anything like that," Maeve said calmly.

"But. . . ." Jerome felt a strong urge to escape from the house, but now the obstinate side of his character was coming to the fore. "I definitely saw it on a shelf, along with some fossils, binoculars and foreign coins. I've got a very good memory for that sort of thing."

"I've got a *terrible* memory for that kind of thing, so why don't we just have a look-see?" Maeve gave a tight smile and opened the door to the sitting room, which looked exactly as he had seen it last time except that the square of hardboard had been replaced over the hole in the floor. "I don't want to use this room again until the floor is fixed, and I'm not allowed to get it done until the coroner's office says."

"I understand." Jerome went past her and walked straight to the bookshelf where he had seen the unusual box. All the other items he remembered were in place, but of the heart-shaped box there was no sign. He scanned the rest of the room then turned to look at Maeve, who was regarding him with watchful interest.

"Don't look at me like that," she protested humorously. "I haven't hidden anything."

Jerome could think of no reason for her to lie. "I don't understand this. Has anybody else been in the room?"

"Nobody."

"Are you certain?"

"Of course I'm certain. I don't get so many callers that I lose track of them."

"It doesn't add up," Jerome said, his bafflement increasing. "The box was sitting right here yesterday."

47

He went on to give a detailed description of the missing object, and when asked to explain his interest reluctantly outlined the theory about the common factor in SHC incidents. He did so in a self-deprecating manner which was intended to ward off criticism, but to his own ears the theory sounded ludicrous in the extreme. The British word "barmy" kept flickering in his mind as he spoke, making his delivery increasingly hesitant. There were further distractions in the form of Maeve's polite incredulity and his niggling annoyance over the fate of the little box. He knew he had seen it, and yet he was almost positive that Maeve was not lying to him—which constituted a minor mystery as insoluble as the central issue of the fire death. His cue to leave came when he saw she was finding it difficult to suppress a yawn.

"I'd better go," he said, wishing he could have made a full search of the room.

Maeve was apologetic. "I'm not usually as droopy as this, but the pill I took last night seems to. . . ." She paused, looking surprised. "I've just remembered something."

"About the box?"

"No—it's just that Doctor Pitman was here yesterday afternoon. I'd forgotten about it, but then I don't class him as a visitor."

Jerome felt a furtive excitement. "Was he your father's physician?"

"Yes, but. . . ."

"Did he come into this room?"

"Yes, but he isn't a thief, if that's what you're trying to imply."

"I'm not implying anything," Jerome said placatingly. "Listen, Maeve—I hope you don't mind me addressing you as Maeve—I *know* how weak this idea about medication is, but if we're ever going to find out what happened to your father we've got to check out all theories, even if it's only to eliminate them one by one. Now, do you know where I can find Doctor Pitman?"

"I do, but I'm not telling you." Maeve walked determinedly into the hall, bringing Jerome with her. "Doctor Pitman is a fine man. He came here yesterday, without even being called, just to make sure I was all right and to give me his condolences—and now you want to go to his home and accuse him of stealing some dumb little box."

"I've forgotten all about the box,' Jerome lied. "All I want to do is ask the doctor if he prescribed any unusual drugs for your father."

Maeve opened the front door, creating a rectangle of multicoloured brilliance. "Mr Jerome, when I contacted the *Examiner* it was to let the people of this town know that my father wasn't a whisky soak. It was *not* to launch you on a new career as a fantasy writer, busybody and general nuisance— and if I hear of you annoying Doctor Pitman I'll complain to your editor and do my best to get you sacked."

A few seconds later, without his being sure of how it had come about, Jerome found himself alone outside the house. During their first meeting Maeve Starzynski had claimed to be quick-tempered, and now he knew exactly what she meant. Something about the tone of her voice warned him that she was not inclined to idle threats, that she was quite capable of going to Anne Kruger and demanding his dismissal. As he went sideways down the high steps, easing the strain on his left knee, it came to him that anybody with a normal quota of commonsense would drop the matter right there. The trouble was that he was no longer in control of his actions. The quiet egotist in him had heard just enough to become an obsessional taskmaster whose orders simply had to be obeyed.

Jerome got into his car, selected "DIRECTORY" on the communications panel and asked for Pitman's home address. A second later the machine said, "Four-eight-four Hampshire Drive, Albany, Whiteford."

Jerome nodded in satisfaction and drove off. Albany was an exclusive enclave where, as a kind of reaction to the strict grid pattern of the rest of the town, the roads had been laid out in meandering curves and given English county names instead of numbers. It took him several minutes to get there and to locate the address on a tree-lined avenue where the houses could only be glimpsed behind banks of shrubbery. He drove into the first opening of a semi-circular drive and stopped outside a substantial brick-built house which was clothed in Persian ivy. The doors of the adjacent garage were open and he could see that it was empty—first intimation that the doctor was not at home.

Jerome went to the front entrance and pressed a white ceramic button set in a ring of antique brass. Chimes sounded within, but nobody came to the door. Unable to face the idea of being brought to a standstill in his investigation he pressed the button again and again, straining his ears for a response. More than a minute went by and the only movement was the flowing and fragmenting of his own reflection in the pebbled glass of the door. Jerome was about to admit defeat when a man's voice came from directly behind him, stopping his breath.

"Doctor Bob ain't here," it said.

Jerome turned quickly and saw a young man who was dressed in work clothes and carrying garden shears. He was almost bald, a few wisps of colourless hair lying across his scalp, and his complexion had the silty colouration which comes when very pale skin is overlaid with a tan. Jerome received the impression that the young man was no stranger to illness.

"Can you tell me where the doctor is?" he said. "Do I need to go to the Medical Arts Building?"

"Hell no, you don't need to do nothin' like that." The young man laughed as though Jerome had made some comical blunder. "Doctor Bob only drove over to Mason's to pick out some new shirts for himself. Ten, fifteen minutes should take care of it."

"In that case I'll wait in my car."

"What you wanna do a thing like that for? You'll melt away

50

to a grease spot in there 'fore long. You come round here and I'll show you where to wait." The young man beckoned to Jerome and without waiting for his reaction walked away and passed out of sight at the side of the house. Jerome followed him to the rear of the premises where there was a sizeable and well-tended garden which featured box hedges and beds of white roses.

"You go in there and take a seat." The young man indicated open French windows leading to a shady room which was furnished as a study or office. "You make yourself comfortable in there."

"I don't think I. . . ." Jerome hesitated, seeking a tactful way to explain that he was loth to enter the room on the authority of a gardener.

"It's okay, it's okay," the young man said, unoffended. "All you got to say is Sammy Birkett gave you the okay. Doctor Bob leaves all this kinda thing to me. Honest."

"Thank you, Sammy." Jerome went into the coolness of the house and sat on a leather chair facing a knee-hole desk. The patient sound of shears from the garden showed that Birkett had resumed work. The walls of the room were largely taken up by floor-to-ceiling bookcases filled with a mixture of medical texts and general works. Between the bookcases were dozens of framed certificates, old family photographs and pale mezzotints of sporting scenes. A chess table sat in front of a slate fireplace. It was the kind of room which had either vanished from the electronic age or was consciously maintained for status reasons, but Jerome sensed it was Pitman's natural working environment and he found himself predisposed to like the doctor.

He waited for ten minutes and then, becoming edgy, got up and examined the photographs in the hope of identifying Pitman. In several of the groups was a likely candidate—a white-haired, apple-cheeked figure in a conservative black suit—but there were no captions to confirm his guess. As the minutes continued to slip by Jerome, although still in the grip

51

of his compulsion, began to be oppressed by mental images of Anne Kruger's face, each time looking angrier than before. Feelings of panic gripped him every time he remembered he was risking his job by being in Pitman's house, and what made matters worse was that he had no genuine hope of having his theory proved right. It was just that he had to have it proved *wrong* before he would be his own man again.

His mounting agitation drove Jerome to prowl around the room, and it was on his third circuit that he observed the envelope with the semi-circular stamp in a waste bin beside the desk. The only source he knew for stamps of that shape was Amity, the USA/UK condominium in the Antarctic. Never having actually seen one of the stamps, Jerome picked up the envelope and was surprised to note that it had come from the Amity headquarters of CryoCare Incorporated.

In the last decade there had been renewed interest in the freeze-preservation of disease victims in the old hope that medical science would one day be able to revive and cure them. CryoCare maintained a body storage and research facility in the Antarctic, where natural conditions aided the work, but in spite of undeniable progress the whole venture was suspect in Jerome's eyes. He had an instinctive distrust of any scheme which involved people in mortal fear being separated from large sums of money. Pitman having dealings with CryoCare hardly squared with the picture Jerome had formed of a benevolent family doctor of the old school, but perhaps the envelope had contained nothing more than promotional literature. Frowning, Jerome dropped it back into the waste bin and walked to the window.

The young gardener was just a few paces away. He had paused in his work and was staring into the distance, his head tilted as if he were straining to hear faint voices. Again Jerome received the impression that Birkett had been battling against illness or was recovering from an operation. He studied the young man sympathetically, suddenly appreciative of the fact that his own ailments could have been much worse. Birkett, unaware of being observed, tucked his shears under his arm and took a small box from the hip pocket of his jeans. He opened it and removed a pill-sized object which he put in his mouth.

Jerome, whose corrected vision was good, recognized the box at once by its distinctive colouration. The scene seemed to flow outwards from the fleck of violet as though his eyes were performing a high-powered zoom, then he was out of the house and striding across the short expanse of patio.

"Sammy," he said breathlessly, abandoning all notions about propriety, "what kind of pill did you just take?"

"Pill?" Birkett gaped at him for a moment and began to smile. "Hell, this ain't no pill." He bared his teeth further, precariously gripping in them a small peach-coloured confection. There was the scent of cinnamon on his breath.

Jerome, abruptly restored to the world of rationality, was both deflated and embarrassed. "I . . . I'm sorry."

"What for?" Birkett said, unconscious of anything odd in Jerome's behaviour, and handed him the box. "These is good. Help yourself."

"Thank you." Jerome examined the box and saw that in spite of its unusual shape it was a mass-produced item. The lid bore the words *Regency Cachous*, and in smaller print: *T. J. Grant & Co., Chipping Norton, Oxford*. He opened the box and tried one of the cachous. Its spiciness brought a feeling of warmth to his tongue, but it was highly unlikely, he told himself—now bitterly self-critical—that sucking it would cause him to burst into flames. He had built a ridiculous edifice of fantasy on a small-town doctor's avuncular habit of distributing confections to his patients.

"Doctor Bob gets 'em all the way from the Old Country," Birkett said, taking the box and replacing it in his pocket. "Full carton at a time. He says they's good for the stomach."

"I'm sure he's absolutely right." Jerome glanced at his watch and quailed as he saw it was only five minutes before 11.00. He had behaved like an idiot, but had been fortunate that he had learned the truth without having spoken to Pitman or having identified himself to the gardener. If he got to the office quickly and gave a plausible excuse for being late the whole ludicrous episode might be safely buried, and with any luck it would be years before he experienced a similar mental aberration.

"Sammy, I've decided not to wait for the doctor," he said. "I'll contact him another time."

Birkett looked concerned. "He'll be back any minute. It don't take him long to pick out shirts."

"It's all right—it was nothing urgent."

"You should make goddamn sure about that." Birkett moved forward unexpectedly and gripped Jerome's arm. "You gotta look out for your health."

"I'll do that," Jerome said, made acutely uncomfortable by the physical contact with a stranger who was beginning to seem more than a little disturbed.

"Doctor Bob will fix you up good." Birkett tightened his grip and when he spoke again it was with an expression of ingenuous pride. "I've got cancer."

"I'm sorry to hear that," Jerome said unhappily, realizing it had been made even more difficult for him to depart quickly. There was a strange protocol to such things.

"I'm gonna be fine, though. Just fine. Doctor Bob is fixin' me up good, even though I got no money for the treatment. That's why I tend his garden. I got no money, but I got a green thumb and I'm a good worker. I keep the garden lookin' good."

"You certainly do." Jerome eased the young man's fingers off his arm, but decided to risk staying an extra few minutes. Birkett seemed hungry for conversation and, in spite of his protestations, was possibly afraid for his life. If Pitman arrived in the meantime it should be possible to concoct a cover story for his visit. Jerome led off by asking Birkett's advice on the cultivation of roses and walked further into the garden with him to examine prime specimens. Finally, deciding he had

54

met his obligations, Jerome made a show of consulting his watch.

"I've enjoyed talking to you, Sammy," he said, "but now I really must go."

Birkett did not reply. He was standing in the attitude in which Jerome had seen him earlier, his sparsely-covered head raised and tilted as if in response to a distant call. His eyes were unfocused, and it was obvious he had not heard Jerome's words. Jerome began to feel trapped. He debated simply turning and hurrying out to his car, but in an indefinable way he had accepted responsibility for the gardener's welfare and he had an uneasy conviction that a crisis was on hand. He looked all about him, desperate for inspiration, and saw that they were close to a small, open-fronted summerhouse.

"Sammy, I think you ought to sit down," he said. "Then I'll get you a glass of water."

He grasped Birkett's arm and urged him towards the white-painted structure. Birkett offered no resistance. Still without speaking, he stumbled alongside Jerome to the summerhouse and sat down on a wooden bench, his back to the inner wall. His eyes stared straight ahead, unseeingly, and his posture was that of an outsized doll propped in a corner.

"I'll be back in a few seconds." Jerome took several paces towards the main house, then turned back as he heard Birkett give a deep retching moan. "Are you going to be all right?"

Gazing strickenly into Jerome's eyes, Birkett opened his mouth and emitted a writhing, roaring tongue of blue flame.

Jerome sank to his knees, both hands pressed to his heart, unable to avert his gaze, groaning an instinctive animal protest at a spectacle which was an affront to reason and the whole of creation. A human being was burning like an oil-soaked torch. Mercifully the enclosed space of the summerhouse filled with dense blue smoke which obscured detail, but Jerome saw enough to germinate a thousand bad dreams. He saw bright fire spread radially from the gaping mouth to annihilate the face. He saw the torso swell, collapse and swell up again as it

55

was consumed by a terrible heat which, miraculously, was slow to ignite the constraining clothes. He saw the nastic twitching of the limbs as they were consumed, turning the body into an obscenely dancing puppet. . . .

Jerome had entered a timeless dimension of horror, but a tiny cowering fragment of his mind was aware that the reduction of Sammy Birkett to crackling cinder was taking place at an incredible speed. A minute went by . . . perhaps two . . . then the visitation was over.

The fire had done its work and had departed.

Still in the kneeling position, Jerome waited for the painful jolting of his heart to subside. When it seemed certain that he too was not going to die he stood up. A shrieking silence had descended over the garden and was cupped in the high perimeter hedges. He moved forward timidly. The blue smoke was dispersing with rapidity, billowing out on a light breeze which brought the sweet stench of it to Jerome's nostrils. He tried to turn himself into a visual recording machine, a dispassionate observer.

The scene in the summerhouse was one of his SHC reference photographs translated into sickening three-dimensional reality. Of Birkett's head and torso there remained only a fine ash heaped in a depression which had been charred into the thick wood of the bench. An incredible degree of heat would have been needed to achieve the degree of destruction in so short a time, and yet the typical SHC anomalies were present. The timber of the summerhouse was dry, but it had not caught alight—and there were large unburnt scraps of the dead man's blue checkered shirt mingled with the ashes.

The legs of Birkett's jeans had also survived as two tubes of material crumpled on the floor, although the flesh and bone inside them had all but vanished, wasted to a powdery residue. Jerome could almost have surmised that the victim had been a mannikin woven from straw or some other equally flammable material had it not been for the other classical feature of the scene. Birkett's hands—all too human—were lying on the

56

bench, one on either side of the mound of ash. Fire had severed them at the wrists and had cauterized the blood vessels in the process, but one of the black cross-sections had cracked and was oozing crimson.

Suddenly Jerome had had enough. His nervous system had been savaged by shock, by grisly images and nauseous smells, and now it had begun to react. He turned away from the abomination in the summerhouse and was violently sick. The first irresistible heave voided his stomach, yet spasm after spasm followed in seemingly endless succession until he had to clutch a nearby sapling for support. And his mind, as though taking action to distance itself from the bodily turmoil, began to fashion cold, clear thoughts:

Spontaneous human combustion was an extremely rare event. Only a few cases were reported worldwide in any given year, without any discernible pattern. It was, therefore, highly remarkable for two residents of the same small town to be stricken within a week of each other.

And it was even more remarkable that both had been receiving treatment from the same physician. . . .

Jerome pushed himself away from the tree and—still retching, but impelled by a thunderous sense of urgency—ran towards his car. He had been searching for a link between fire deaths, for a common factor, but he had not considered a human agency.

And he was not prepared for an encounter with the enigmatic Doctor Pitman.

Chapter 4

As soon as he reached home Jerome washed his face with cold water and brushed his teeth to rid himself of the lingering aftertaste of bile.

It was half an hour before noon and the house and its furnishings had a faint air of unfamiliarity. At first he put it down to something like the insomnia effect, to his being home at an unusual time, then he realized there had been a shift in his perception of the entire universe. *Everything* seemed slightly alien to him now that he had seen the unthinkable happen. On the previous day he had become convinced that spontaneous human combustion was a reality, but the knowledge had been isolated in his head. Now he knew about the fire death in his heart and guts, as part of his direct experience, and there was the problem of adjusting to a world in which such things could occur.

He was also conscious of significant changes affecting the phenomenon itself. The entire history of SHC had been characterized by lack of pattern, by a sheer randomness which defeated all attempts to find an underlying mechanism. There had been only one previous occasion when it had seemed that a hint of order might be introduced and that had been as far back as 1938. On April 7th of that year three men—one near Nijmegen in Holland, one near Chester in England and one on a ship steaming south of Ireland—had become classic examples of SHC at exactly the same time. But the simultaneity of their deaths had only served to add mystery to mystery. There had been no more visible correlations until the deaths of Art Starzynski and Sammy Birkett and now the pendulum had swung the other way.

Jerome had no hesitation in ruling out coincidence, which meant that Doctor Pitman was starkly revealed as a connecting link. For hundreds of years the fire death had preserved its essential mystery—but now, suddenly, the phenomenon was yielding secrets to an amateur investigator. Jerome frowned, took off his glasses and began to polish the lenses as he considered the implications. The assumption of mediocrity guided researchers in fields as diverse as cosmology and particle physics. All egotism gone, burned away in the flame which had devoured Birkett, he had to accept that he was no more gifted than any of the countless others who had pitted themselves against the riddle of SHC, and yet—unless his conclusion about Pitman was totally false—he had made a major breakthrough in little more than a day. Either he was fantastically lucky, or the parameters of the problem were changing.

What the hell am I trying to say? Jerome demanded of himself irritably. *Why am I trying to tie extra knots in the string?*

He put his glasses on again and his gaze steadied on the modest collection of liquor bottles on the living room sideboard. They had scarcely been touched since Carla's death, but the clean taste of gin might help to restore a feeling of sanity to his world. It might also quell the tremors which had been coursing through him since he had watched Birkett's face burn outwards from the mouth.

He mixed a gin and club soda and, not bothering to fetch ice, sat down to marshal his thoughts. An idea to be considered was that in yielding to sheer fright he had proved himself completely inept as a reporter. Any newsman with courage and the right instincts would have seized the opportunity to make a name for himself—and there was still time for Jerome to do the same. The chances were that Birkett's remains had not yet been discovered in the seclusion of the summerhouse. All Jerome had to do was go back there, telephone the police, start filing sensational and highly profitable stories with major news agencies, stir up a hornets' nest.

Sipping his drink, he tried to imagine himself facing up to

59

Doctor Pitman, hard-nosing his way through all the consequent furore, and his mood altered for the worse as he realized he was not up to it. The next best thing would be to call Anne Kruger and turn everything over to her, but even that much seemed beyond him. He was gripped by a numb timidity. Given a free choice he would have run for cover, perhaps to the privacy and safety of the chalet at Parson's Lake.

Wondering if his feelings were a typical aftermath of shock, Jerome made a conscious effort to induce relaxation while he was finishing his drink. His heart beat was alternating between birdlike flutters and periods of suspenseful pounding. He was reluctant to believe that the tightness he had recently been experiencing in his chest after exertion was anything to worry about, but it seemed advisable to calm down as thoroughly as possible and think clearly about his next move. The problem lay with the problem—because it *had* changed, almost beyond recognition.

He was reminded of the way in which a decaying smoke ring can still be seen as a torus long after a newcomer to the room would observe only formless ribbons drifting in the air. The great enigma of SHC remained, but its outlines were being distorted by a more urgent question—if latching on to Doctor Pitman or an equivalent elsewhere was so easy why had nobody done it before? And that question led directly to another. Was he, in his heart, attributing sinister motives to Pitman? An obvious interpretation of events was that an innocently prescribed drug, or a rare combination of drugs, had led to freakish tragedies—but Jerome's subconscious mind seemed to have other. . . .

The buzzing of the telephone made him flinch. He stared at it for a few seconds, knowing that the caller was his editor or a deputy, then got out of his chair and picked up the instrument. Anne Kruger wasted no time on preliminaries.

"Just tell me one thing," she said. "Is this Thursday?"

As always, her brand of heavy sarcasm needled him. "Let's see. Yesterday was Wednesday, so—unless there's been a drastic revision in the calendar—it's safe to assume that this. . . ."

"Don't try to be funny, Ray."

You started it, he thought. "What can I do for you, Anne?"

"Have you considered writing news stories?"

"That's what I'm doing," Jerome said. "I can concentrate better at home."

"Oh? And what red-hot page-one lead are you concentrating on at the moment?"

Only an eyewitness account of a second SHC death! Go on, man, say it! Tell her about the two fire deaths clearly linked by the same doctor. Boost yourself to the skies in her estimation. Make a name for yourself in journalism. . . .

"Ah . . . well . . . it's a bit difficult for me to. . . ." Jerome was appalled to hear himself begin to stammer. "I'm still organizing my notes for the Starzynski piece."

"*Still!* Have you done anything about the new pictures?"

"Not yet. You see. . . ."

"Forget about the pictures," Anne cut in, her voice cold. "I'll put Cordwell on to that side of it. You, my friend, have an entire page of this newspaper to fill, and you've got two hours in which to do it. I advise you to start writing immediately because I'm going to be watching your copy come in. And if it doesn't come in, *you* needn't come in either. Not *ever*. Got that?" The telephone clicked and began a complacent purring.

Jerome gave a shaky laugh as he set the phone down. His first reaction was indignation over the way Anne had spoken to him, but a moment's reflection told him he deserved all he had got, plus a lot more. He had won the position with the *Examiner* on the strength of having been part-time editor of an engineering society journal, and he liked to think he brought unusual and valuable attributes to the job, but events were proving just how shallow his conceits were. Any sub-literate dolt dragged out of a pool hall would have been more useful to the newspaper than a reporter who did not report.

Why had he not simply opened his mouth and told Anne

61

about Birkett's death? Furthermore, what was stopping him from phoning her back and belatedly putting things right?

Jerome looked down at the telephone and experienced something close to panic as he realized that, not only was he quite incapable of picking it up, he could not face the prospect of being in range of it for the rest of the day. It was an open gateway through which anybody could invade his home, and what he needed was a period of undisturbed peace in which to pull himself together. A vision of the chalet at Parson's Lake flickered briefly in his mind. Invitingly.

Suppressing a pang of shame, he allowed himself to consider the idea of simply running away to the country for a few days. It would be an immature and irresponsible action, one which was quite likely to cost him his job, but the lake would guarantee him the tranquillity he so desperately craved. Nobody at the office even knew about the holiday home, so there would be no interruptions, nothing to hinder his attempts to rebuild a rational model of the universe inside his head. Again the image of the low-roofed chalet appeared behind his eyes, so clearly that he could almost smell the pine forest backdrop, and before he could even admit to what was happening he was in the bedroom packing a holdall.

The task occupied little more than five minutes, but he could visualize Anne Kruger already standing by a computer terminal in the *Examiner*'s office, already growing impatient as she waited for his first paragraphs to appear on the screen. All at once nothing in the whole world mattered more to him than escaping from the house before the telephone rang again. He grabbed the tartan bag, strode to the front door and, pausing only to switch on the burglar alarm, went out into the noon sunshine. The avenue, with its glowing lawns and wine-coloured shingle roofs, was a picture of placid normality— except, Jerome reminded himself, any of its inhabitants might suddenly burst into flame. Anybody who had newly acquired that burden of knowledge was entitled to go into retreat for as long as he wanted. He got into his car, slinging his bag on to

62

the seat beside him, and drove in the direction of the state highway which would take him west.

Fifteen minutes out of Whiteford he noticed that his fuel tank was registering quarter full, the level at which he always filled up again. His sense of urgency had not lessened, but old habits prevailed. He pulled into a self-service station he had used several times in the past and which derived most of its business from local farmers. There was the usual cluster of dust-streaked cars and pick-ups parked outside the adjoining lunch counter, and he could see a mechanic at work beneath a car in the maintenance bay. Nobody here was worried about abruptly torching up, burning outwards from the mouth.

Jerome got out of the car, fed a credit card into a pump and began filling his tank. He had been watching the gaseous shimmering around the nozzle for only a few seconds when he developed the uncomfortable conviction that somebody was staring at him. He turned his head and saw, some ten paces away, a man of about thirty dressed in hunting clothes. The man had a city-dweller's pallor which contrasted oddly with his sports garb, but something about him proclaimed abundant physical strength. He continued openly staring at Jerome with an expression which suggested mild contempt.

Puzzled and irritated, wondering if he could be straying into a bad day at Black Rock situation, Jerome opened his mouth to ask what the stranger found so interesting in him. Then he thought better of it. He was no fighter, and the other man's physical presence was strangely daunting. Trying to be casual about it, Jerome averted his gaze, but not before he had seen the man smile a derisive, pike-mouthed smile which showed only his bottom teeth. Jerome kept his eyes on the dancing ruby numerals of the pump's register and was relieved to hear footsteps moving away in the direction of the service bay. He guessed the man had run into car trouble, was seething over the delay and was taking it out on anybody who went near him.

And if that was a psychological duel, I got whipped, Jerome thought, yearning for the seclusion of Parson's Lake. It had never been a popular location for holiday homes, thanks to the marshy nature of the shore, and the handful of houses that did exist were likely to be empty in midweek. He had been there only once since Carla had died. On that occasion the chalet had felt unbearably lonely, but now it seemed a haven, free from horrors and petty aggressions, a place where a thinking man could contentedly spend the rest of his days. Anxious to complete the journey, he finished pumping gas, retrieved his card and got into the car. A glance at the maintenance bay showed that the disconcerting stranger was watching the mechanic at work on his car. Jerome accelerated out on to the highway, oppressed by a feeling that he had narrowly avoided serious trouble, and settled down for the rest of the sixty kilometre drive.

He made one more stop to buy groceries and reached the lake by early afternoon. The water was an expanse of pure indigo liberally sewn with sun-diamonds and, as he had hoped, there was a stillness in the air which proclaimed absence of people. He stopped the car in the small clearing beside his own chalet and got out, breathing deeply.

His rowboat was in place under its slick cover at the water's edge, awaiting a fresh coat of varnish. That was a job he might tackle to keep his hands busy while he was getting his thoughts together. The house itself, partially hidden by feathery clumps of oleander, seemed to bid him a mute welcome and he congratulated himself on having retained it. Their insurance had fallen far short of meeting the costs of Carla's terminal illness and after her death there had been a big temptation to let the chalet go, but now his decision to keep it was proved good. In fact, if Anne Kruger went as far as firing him and he was forced to cut back, he would incline towards selling the house in Whiteford and retiring to the country.

Already beginning to feel restored and comforted, he took his box of groceries from the trunk of the car and carried them on to the screened verandah. A raised nail made itself felt through the sole of his shoe—another homely chore to be taken care of. He opened the front door with his key, went into the hall and carried the food towards the kitchen at the rear of the house. The living room was on his right. He glanced through its open door as he went by, continued on for two more paces and stopped, frowning, as he identified what was wrong with his eidetic image of the room.

One of the pair of shotguns which usually hung above the fireplace was missing.

Still clasping the weighty cardboard carton, he backtracked and went into the living room. The support brackets were still in place, so the gun had not fallen and bounced out of sight behind a chair. The only other explanation which sprang to mind was that the house had been burgled—but why would a thief not have taken both weapons?

"No, you haven't been robbed," said a man's voice from the innermost corner of the room.

The box slipped from Jerome's arms as he spun to his left and saw the dark-suited, apple-cheeked old man who was holding the missing shotgun. Time almost stopped for Jerome. He saw the box drift towards the floor in slow motion, its contents shifting as they became relatively weightless. He took in and identified every detail of the intruder—the abundant silver hair, the gold watch chain across the vest, the large square hands. He heard the box strike the floor, then came the first sledgehammer beat from his heart. And it *hurt*. There was a roaring in his ears and it seemed that the next heartbeat was never going to come . . .

"Don't be stupid," the old man commanded, laser-eyed. "Be calm, I tell you! Breathe easy!"

Jerome sucked in air, and part of him was dully astonished to feel a curious placidity flood through his system. It was as though a hypodermic of powerful tranquilliser had gone straight into an artery. He backed away from the other man, no longer in shock but in a way more deeply afraid than before.

65

"You're Pitman," he accused. "How did you do that?"

Doctor Pitman gave a paternal smile. "It's easy when you know how. More important, young man, how long is it since you've had a medical check-up?"

"Five or six years. I'm not sure. I don't like having check-ups."

"Why not?"

"They only try to find things wrong. I prefer not to. . . ." Jerome broke off, suddenly outraged by the sheer enormity of what was happening. "What is this? What the hell *is* this? What are you doing in my house?"

"I'm only returning the courtesy, Ray—you were in my house this morning." Pitman continued smiling, showing teeth which still looked healthy in spite of his seventy-odd years. "I thought you wanted to talk to me."

"I did, but. . . ." Jerome resisted an impulse to back away. "There's something wrong here."

"That's good, Ray. You're an intelligent man and your brain is functional again—which will make things easier for both of us. I was concerned about you a minute ago."

"I don't want your concern."

"I know," Pitman said. "What you really want is to find out how I knew about your visit when the only person you met is dead."

Jerome nodded. "That's enough for starters. How *did* you know?"

"It's very simple, Ray." Pitman paused as though for dramatic effect, apparently relishing the moment, like a club bore spinning out a dull story. "I'm telepathic. I can tell what people are thinking."

Jerome almost moaned aloud with relief. All thoughts of Pitman's connection with the horrors of spontaneous human combustion were banished from his mind by the glad realization that he had been totally wrong about the doctor. The strange circumstances of their meeting, the admittedly impressive hypnotic trick with the eyes, the grand manner—all

66

these things had combined to create in him the feeling that the doctor was a near-superman, dangerously gifted. Now he was revealed as yet another crackpot, someone a rational man could outwit and manipulate. The manipulation would have to be done very carefully because of the shotgun, but even with allowances for that the situation was not as bad as he had feared. Pitman was merely holding the gun, not aiming it at him, and in all probability had not even been able to find the shells.

"I did find the shells," Pitman said gently. "The pantry was one of the first places I thought of searching."

Having grasped the lifeline, Jerome had no intention of letting go. "Beautifully done," he said. "I wasn't even aware of glancing at the gun."

"I'm glad you've got a logical turn of mind," Pitman replied. "You must realize, my boy, that my problem has always been the exact opposite of that facing phoney mind-readers. They go to great lengths to convince researchers that they can do things they can't, whereas I've always had to conceal my ability. I've often wondered how long it would take me, should the need arise, to persuade a sceptic that I really am telepathic."

Jerome sniffed. "I doubt if either of us can spare that many decades."

"You've also got a rather acid tongue, haven't you, Ray?" Pitman paused to give Jerome a look of fatherly reproach. "No, I'd say the job could be done in about one minute flat. Happily, the more rational a person is in his scepticism, the harder it is for him to ignore first-class evidence. Isn't that so?"

"You've got the . . . ball." Jerome had been about to mention the gun and had changed his mind on the grounds that it was better to keep the doctor's thoughts on other things. Part of him marvelled at his own resilience, the ease with which he had slipped into a role implanted in his consciousness by a hundred teleplays. He had never dealt with a genuine madman before, but the technique was almost instinctive—play it cool, establish a bond, wait your chance.

"Here you are, Ray—the sort of evidence for which Rhine would have given his right arm." Pitman nodded at the davenport in front of the fireplace. "Perhaps you'd like to sit down?"

Jerome shook his head. "I'll stand."

"Very well. We'll make this very simple. I want you to think of a series of objects and I'll tell you what they are. Is that all right?"

"It's all right with me," Jerome said compliantly, realizing he would be called upon to exercise some nice judgment. Obviously he would have to give the doctor a good score to humour him, but exactly how good could it be before the doctor's suspicions were aroused?

Pitman made an impatient gesture. "Start now. Think of something."

"Sure." Jerome assumed an earnest expression while he dealt with a new worry. Had it all been too easy so far? Insane people could be devious and clever—which meant that Pitman could be setting an elaborate trap. It might very well be that telling him he had correctly divined a thought would send him into a homicidal rage.

"I'm not getting anything," Pitman said sharply. "You must focus your thoughts on some concrete object."

"Sorry—I'm not used to this." Jerome, in the spirit of someone reluctantly joining a childish game, visualized a farm tractor.

Pitman said, "A tractor."

Jerome blinked. He had driven through a lot of farming country to reach Parson's Lake, had seen quite a few tractors, and the doctor must have done the same. The trick was to be less predictable. He pondered for a moment then visualized a New York taxi.

Pitman said, "A yellow cab."

That had been another form of transport, too closely linked to a tractor. Jerome thought again, taking longer this time, and imagined himself looking at the Mona Lisa.

Pitman said, "The Mona Lisa."

The most famous painting in the world. The best-known single object in the world. He should have chosen a really obscure painting—like the faded watercolour of a tea clipper which had hung above the piano in his Aunt May's front room in Albany.

Pitman said, "A picture of a sailing ship."

Transport again—the piano itself would have been better.

Pitman said, "A piano."

Jerome gazed soberly at the doctor for a few seconds and said, "I'd like to sit down now, if you don't mind."

"I think you should." Pitman was no longer smiling. "This has been quite a day for you—and unfortunately it's far from over."

Jerome backed away from the fallen box of provisions and lowered himself on to a bentwood chair near the living room door. He felt strangely calm, considering that his universe had undergone yet another upheaval, but his legs were rubbery. It was something of a relief to find that he could still speak without a tremor in his voice.

"The other thing I was going to ask you was how you found out in advance that I was coming here," he said. "But I guess I already know the answer to that one."

Pitman brought another bentwood out from the wall and straddled it, moving with the litheness of a much younger man. "You only know part of the answer. You see, I gave you the idea of coming here in the first place—and you may be pleased to hear that I also prevented you telling the whole world what happened to Sammy Birkett. I wasn't able to exercise direct control—I'm not that powerful—but I was able to upset your judgment. What it boils down to is you're not as bad at your job as you feared."

"But that's. . . ."

"It isn't impossible, Ray—just difficult. And very tiring. Active telepathy really takes the starch out of me, so I'm glad I don't have to do it too often."

69

"I really don't know if I can cope with this," Jerome said helplessly. "I didn't believe in spontaneous human combustion until yesterday, and I didn't believe in telepathy until a minute ago . . . and now . . . and now you're here with my gun . . . Why do you need the gun, for God's sake?"

"I need it because I may have to kill you," Pitman replied. "I don't want to kill you, and I deeply regret having to speak to you in these terms, but there's so much at stake here that if I can't get your co-operation I'll terminate your life. Is that understood?"

"You make things very clear." Jerome was surprised to discover that he felt a cold gloominess rather than fear. "Is there any point in my uttering the classic line?"

"I *will* get away with it, Ray, and I beg you to stop equating this with a scene from a play. I brought some chains in my car, and in a moment we're going to take your rowboat out to the centre of the lake. There'll be nobody around to hear the shot, nobody to see your body going overboard . . . You've got to take this thing very seriously."

"I'm not laughing," Jerome said. "Look, of course I'll co-operate. I'd be crazy not to. I promise you I'll go along with any plan you have in mind."

"What else could you say?" Pitman stood up and changed his grip on the shotgun, closing his right hand around the trigger guard. "You've got your colour back. I do believe you're fit enough to do a little gentle rowing. Let's go."

Jerome got to his feet and now, suddenly, he was afraid. Deathly afraid. "This part isn't necessary. I swear to you that I'll. . . ."

Pitman shook his head. "Out to the boat, Ray. Move!"

Jerome walked slowly into the hall. The front door was still open and the scene beyond it could have graced a travel brochure—an acrylic composition of water, trees and distance-blued hills, with nothing in it to indicate that the whole world had gone monstrously wrong. Jerome had never been threatened with a firearm before and now he found himself

70

morbidly conscious of the shotgun and all its engineered detail. As he walked out to the verandah he wondered what state of readiness the gun was in. If the doctor had neglected to release the safety catch it might be possible to wrest the weapon from him.

"Don't try it," Pitman said gently. "I've never liked guns, but I know how to use one."

"Is it easy to tell what a person is thinking?"

"When he's thinking graphically—the way you were doing just now."

"I see." Jerome stepped down off the verandah and walked towards his boat. In his mind he conjured up an image of an orange and held it there, trying to make it real, while at another level he thought about the oars lying beneath the boat's covering. An oar would (*see every pore on the orange skin; imagine the smell and the taste*) make an effective club if he could get a good grip on it (*see the oil spurting as your thumb goes into the peel, feel the pith under your nail*) before Pitman realized what he was doing.

"That's not much better," Pitman said. "The orange was too irrelevant, an obvious screen. As soon as it appeared I went underneath. In any case, the oars are too heavy."

"Thanks for the advice," Jerome said, again wondering at his own adaptability. He was numb with dread at the prospect of a tight-packed cloud of lead pellets storming through his body, and yet his mind was swarming with questions about the doctor and his incredible powers. Was Pitman the only telepath in the world, or was he a member of a talented group? Why the secrecy about mind-reading? Fear of pogroms? And, above all, what was the connection with spontaneous human combustion? There had to be a connection—it would have been the ultimate coincidence if the man who linked two SHC cases was also a telepath by sheer chance—but Jerome could not begin to imagine it. Were it not for his worries about being shot he would be in a state of high excitement at the thought of getting some answers.

71

He pulled the weighted plastic cover off the boat and set it aside. A spider scuttled away when he moved the oars, which were lying on the crossbenches. Jerome lifted the spider on the blade of an oar and let it escape on to the ground, and when he turned back to the boat he saw that Pitman was retrieving some chains which had been hidden in the sedge grass.

"Is that all you've got?" Jerome said, hoping to affect the doctor's plans. "A set of snow chains?"

Pitman slung the chains into the boat. "It's enough—a corpse which has been well ventilated doesn't develop much buoyancy."

"Oh." Jerome regretted having brought the subject up. "Is it all a charade, this business about trying to get my co-operation? How do I know you're not planning to pull the trigger regardless of what I say?"

"I give you my word."

"What good is it? Come to that, what good will my word be to you?" Jerome felt he was taking a gamble, but there were issues which had to be settled. "I could promise you anything just to get away from you in one piece, then I could go to the police."

"You couldn't trick *me*," Pitman said. "Remember, I'm the man who can read your mind."

"I still don't see why we have to go out on the lake," Jerome said doggedly. "I can tell you right now that I'm going to agree to anything you propose. That much is obvious, isn't it?"

"No." Pitman was smiling again, but his eyes were unreadable. "Most people would regard what I'm going to ask you to do as . . . well, they would call it betraying the entire human race. It's quite possible that you'll feel the same way, that you simply won't be able to go along with it. Oh, you'll *say* you're going to co-operate, but in your heart you'll know that you can't. Perhaps you'll even be able to deceive yourself, but you won't be able to deceive me. And if that's the way it works out—I'll kill you."

"Jesus!" Jerome gave a dispirited sigh. "And all because I saw what happened to Sammy Birkett?"

"I'm afraid so."

"Can I at least be told why some people burn up?"

"Push the rowboat into the water, Ray—then steady it while I get in."

The boat had bedded itself into the soft ground and Jerome had difficulty shifting it until Pitman put one foot on the stern and thrust with surprising force. The craft became easier to handle as it nuzzled into the water. Keeping the shotgun aimed directly at Jerome's stomach, the doctor stepped into the boat and positioned himself on the aft bench. His movements were easy and economical in spite of his portly form. Jerome, whose arthritic knee was protesting at the effort of dealing with the boat, was chastened to realize that even without the gun the elderly man could probably outmatch him in a struggle. Wincing as the muddy water lapped around his shins, Jerome climbed aboard and used the oars to get the boat free of the rushes and into clear water against a steady breeze. He was breathing hard and the tightness was returning to his chest.

"Row us out to the centre of the lake, but do it gently and don't overexert yourself," Pitman said. "I don't want anything to happen to you."

Jerome tried to sneer. "Unless you do it."

"I understand your feeling that way, but speaking as a medical practitioner I'm advising you to . . . How old are you, anyway?"

"Fifty," Jerome snapped. "How old are you?"

An enigmatic expression appeared on Pitman's face. "The body you're looking at is seventy-six years of age. I am almost thirty years older."

Jerome considered the statement. "Talk sense."

"I'm sorry," Pitman said, looking genuinely contrite. "This is so difficult. What would you say if I told you I wasn't born on Earth?"

"I'd say you were a spaceman."

"Pejorative use of the word, I think, but this is the truth—I was born on a different planet."

"One I would know about?"

"My people's name for it is Dorrin." Pitman's gaze was steady. "But you know it as Mercury."

"I see." Jerome felt appreciably relieved. He had made the mistake of underestimating Pitman where telepathy was concerned and since then had been psychologically disadvantaged at every turn, but at last there had come a development which offered some hope. The doctor still had the upper hand, but if he was deluded enough to believe he was an extraterrestrial that was evidence of a weakness of mind which might be exploited. Jerome thought briefly of the utterly barren, radiation-scoured surface of Mercury, familiar to him from photographs, then with an effort of will changed his visualization to that of an Earth-bound astronomer. He pictured a soft speck of light almost lost in the afterglow of sunset.

"I don't know much about Mercury," he said, trying to strike the right note of credulity. "Is it a pleasant place?"

"It's a hellish place, as you very well know," Pitman replied. "I told you before, Ray—there's no point in trying to fool me."

"All right, I just can't see how any life could have evolved in a place like that."

Pitman shook his head. "There was no evolution. Both Earth and Mercury were colonized by human space travellers from another star system. It happened so long ago that we have no records of which star our ancestors came from, or why they were attracted to Mercury in the first place. It was hardly an obvious choice for colonization, even though its synchronous rotation meant there was a fairly habitable twilight zone."

Got you! Jerome thought triumphantly. *Your knowledge of your so-called home planet is about forty years out of date.* For an instant he was tempted to remain quiet, to encourage the doctor to make more elementary blunders, then he thought better of it. Pitman reacted badly to insincerity.

Jerome cleared his throat and said, "I hate to drag in an awkward fact, but. . . ."

"But Mercury does rotate in respect to the Sun. That fact isn't awkward, my boy—it's tragic. When Mercury was colonized it *was* in captured rotation, keeping one hemisphere away from the Sun, and the Dorrinian people were able to exist there in relative comfort. Our cities were underground, of course, and we had to manufacture our own atmosphere, but the system was viable and stable—until the Days of the Comet."

"Ah, yes," Jerome said. "H. G. Wells."

Pitman sighed his disapproval. "That tongue of yours must cost you a lot of friends."

"My friends don't aim shotguns at me."

"Point acknowledged, but it's in your own interests to take what I'm saying very seriously. I advise you to keep quiet and absorb the information."

"Go on." Jerome rowed in a slow rhythm, the familiar activity pointing up the bizarre nature of the situation. The sunlight was intensely bright on the open stretch of lake and Pitman was delineated with a kind of luminous clarity against a background made up of horizontal bands of water, hushed trees, blue-green hills and sky. With his broad, benign countenance, silver hair and conservative business suit he should have been behind a desk, posing for a let-me-be-your-father advertising shot, instead of sitting in a rowboat with a gun on his knee, interlarding expressions of concern with death threats, fact with fantasy. . . .

"More than three thousand Earth years ago—in the 15th century BC to be precise—a very large comet blundered into the solar system," Pitman went on, the intensity of his gaze warning Jerome to remain silent.

"It was drawn into the Sun, brushing close by Mercury on the way and imparting to it the spin which is now observed by Earth astronomers, one revolution every fifty-eight Earth days. That was a catastrophe for the Dorrinians, who found the former temperate zone being blasted by the full radiation of the Sun. Most of them died before they could go far enough

75

underground to find shelter. Even those who did survive were hard-pressed to stay alive, because the Sun's heat penetrated farther into the planetary crust with each new rotation. It is estimated that ninety per cent of the Dorrinian population was lost in the Days of the Comet."

Jerome nodded, not trusting himself to make any comment. It had taken him a moment to understand why he had found Pitman's reference to the 15th century BC significant, then his memory had stirred into action. Immanuel Velikovsky, perhaps the crankiest pseudo-scientist of all, had assigned that dating to his giant comet which was supposed to have grazed Earth and caused a number of Biblical "miracles". In Velikovsky's scenario the comet had eventually settled down to become the planet Venus, but here it was careering onwards into the Sun and on the way playing havoc with a civilization on Mercury. Pitman's story had the classical attributes of all such fanciful edifices, which were grab-bags of anything which could be filched from other disciplines to mask their essential implausibility. It appeared that being a telepath, assuming the doctor genuinely had the ability, was no defence against eccentricity—but there still remained the enigma of his connection with the fire death. . . .

"You're not paying attention, Ray," Pitman reproved. "You should mark the fact that Dorrinian science has evolved differently from that of Earth. The sheer lack of physical resources forced us to concentrate on our mental abilities. We are weak on hard technology and engineering, but we have compensated with our progress on mind-to-mind and mind-to-matter interactions. I have already given you proof of that."

"I admit I was impressed back there in the house," Jerome said, deciding to risk open scepticism as a way to keep the doctor talking, "but I've just thought of a non-psi explanation."

"You'd better verbalize it—I can't read the melange of blurry abstracts in your mind."

Jerome forced a smile. "That's neat. Look, I freely concede

76

that you're an excellent hypnotist—you proved it when you *commanded* me to get over the shock I had when I found you in the house with a gun."

"Continue."

"Well, I've also seen a lot of astonishing things done with post-hypnotic commands. You could easily have ordered me to *say* the name of any object I pictured in my mind, and also to be unaware that I was saying it. And there you have it—a totally convincing demonstration of telepathy."

"That's quite . . . ingenious," Pitman said. "How do people like you learn to think that way?"

"It was started a long time ago by a character called William of Occam."

Pitman frowned. "Does Occamism explain why I would go to such lengths to deceive you?"

"Who knows why a. . . .?" Jerome checked himself, aware that he was again straying into dangerous territory.

"Why a crank does anything?" The index finger of Pitman's right hand slid off the gun's trigger guard and curled around the trigger itself. "I can't really be angry at you, Ray. The so-called rationalist mode of thought has saved my people from exposure time after time when one of us has accidentally given himself away. We've had reason to be grateful to your ability to blind yourselves to the obvious, but in this case . . . I wonder if I should stop wasting my valuable time on you."

"I promised there'd be no tricks," Jerome said, dry-mouthed. "That involved speaking my mind, voicing honest doubts—and I've just thought of something else."

"Out with it."

"I couldn't fault your telepathy demonstration if it was done over again in front of my video camera."

"I've got a better idea," Pitman said, laser-eyed. "Try your Occam's Razor on this."

Jerome knew several kinds of pain.

There was the straightforward physical pain of neural over-load, centred on his brain. . . .

There was the unmanning psychological pain, shot through with terror, of having another personality enter the temple of his own flesh, dispossessing him, perhaps for ever. . . .

And there was the spiritual pain, the blighting of the soul with sadness and vain regrets, brought on when Nature practises one of her careless genocides on one's own race. He saw Dorrinian men, women and children die in their millions. He took part in the agonizingly slow retreat to the depths of the planetary crust, while yet more of his kind perished with each awesome transit of the Sun. . . .

There could be no physical escape to Earth for those who survived, but Jerome was vicariously present when the Dorrinian grand plan was conceived and executed. It took generations of selective breeding before the first super-telepaths appeared—individuals who could mentally reach out across space and by sheer concentration of will install their own personalities in Terran bodies. Jerome observed and took part in the surreptitious invasion of Earth, the slow, silent invasion which had been going on for more than three thousand years. . . .

The linen tape binding the oar handle was shiny in places, blackened with use, but when one stared hard at the blackness the warp and weft of the material could still be seen inside it, like a microscopic grid of ivory inlaid in jet. Jerome gazed at the handle for a long time, trying to work out what it was, then he raised his head and made his eyes focus on Doctor Pitman.

He said, "That wasn't fair."

Pitman was unruffled. "You're a hard man to reach, Ray. Quiet arrogance is the worst kind."

"Even so. . . ." Jerome felt dizzy and sick, suspended between two realities. "How many of you are there on Earth?"

"Not many. A very small proportion of Dorrinians have the required ability. Volunteers for the transfer usually have to spend days preparing themselves, taking special drugs, building up the necessary potential. Even then it's a hazardous operation. Even for a super-telepath it is *extremely* difficult to locate the emanations from one target kald among the billions that are broadcasting on Earth."

"Kald?" Jerome had an uneasy sense of having learned the word and forgotten it a thousand years earlier.

"There's no equivalent in Earth languages," Pitman said. "Kald is the Dorrinian word for the entire human entity—not just the body or the mind, but the complex of body, nervous system, brain, mind, spirit, personality and all the associated energy fields. Telepathy is partly a physical process, you see, and that's what makes the Dorrin-to-Earth transfer so dangerous."

There was an icy upheaving in Jerome's subconscious. "Is this anything to do with SHC?"

"Unfortunately—yes. You can think of the kald as being like a flexible lens existing on several levels of reality. The analogy is greatly simplified, you understand, but when a Dorrinian is making a transfer to Earth that lens is adjusted to a focal length equal to the distance between the two worlds. And a lens is a two-way system. There is a narrow cone of influence reaching from Dorrin to Earth, and an opposing counterpart stretching back towards. . . ."

"The Sun!" The gentle movement of the boat beneath Jerome could have been a rocking of the physical horizon.

"That's correct." Pitman's voice was quiet and matter-of-fact, his words quickly fading away into the lake's surrounding stillness. "Transfers are completely impossible when Mercury as seen from Earth is near the Sun. They are best achieved when Mercury is at its maximum elongation. That's the safest time, but there's no guarantee that something won't go wrong. The Dorrinian may lose control for internal reasons, or there may be a continuum disturbance, or there may be a malign . . . well, let's not go into that . . .

"The consequence is that for an instant the kald lens is disrupted. The needle cones of influence fan out into oscillating hemispheres which encompass the Sun, and solar heat is funnelled into the target body. And people on Earth—the few who choose to pay attention, that is—have another case of spontaneous human combustion to marvel at."

"I . . . But. . . ." Jerome suddenly realized he had nothing to say. It was partly an after-effect of his telepathic excursion into the Dorrinian racial consciousness, partly the shock value of what he had just heard, but he found himself overwhelmed, unable to cope with the torrent of new concepts.

"The people who *were* interested in recent decades have been using computers in their search for patterns in the incidence of SHC," Pitman continued, almost as though talking for his own benefit. "They've had hundreds of dates to feed into their playthings, and I kept waiting for somebody to notice that no case had ever been reported when Mercury was in line with or close to the Sun. That regular trough has been clearly visible in the data right from the beginning, but nobody caught on. Can't really blame them. Thinking in other categories is all very well, but you can't help unconsciously setting a limit. What do you say, my boy?"

"I've just understood why you talked about my betraying the whole race," Jerome said, aimlessly trailing his oars in the water. "From what you told me, we only get to know about these transfers of yours that go wrong. Presumably a much greater number of transfers take place *without* anything going wrong . . . and . . . and the word transfer is a euphemism, isn't it? It's another way of saying murder."

Jerome stared at Pitman, wondering how he had brought himself to go so far, surprised to discover that anger and resentment can be more persuasive than fear. All scepticism had been banished from his mind and he now understood the doctor's earlier cryptic remark about being thirty years older than his body. It meant that the physical form of Robert Pitman, exuding its manicured reassurance and Rotary Club respectability, actually housed a member of an alien race.

Apparently the Dorrinians felt they were entitled to use their mind science and psi-powers as weapons against the ordinary people of Earth, but whether an Art Starzynski or a

Sammy Birkett burned up with solar heat in a failed transfer or simply had his personality erased, the end result was the same. It amounted to nothing less than murder. The Dorrinians could no more be justified than invaders using bomb or bayonet—and Jerome resented their actions. He resented their alien presence so passionately that there was no point in his trying to disguise the fact, either from Pitman or from himself.

"I never thought I'd hear myself saying a thing like this," he told Pitman, "but you might as well pull the trigger right now and get it over with. I don't need to tell you the reason, do I?"

"There isn't much reasoning going on in that skull of yours at the moment," Pitman said, beginning to sound exasperated. "The Dorrinians are a highly ethical people who revere life above all else. Would we be having this long and increasingly tedious conversation if I were a murderer?"

"Ethical?" Jerome glanced meaningfully at the shotgun. "Do tell me all about ethics."

Pitman consulted his gold watch, sighed and replaced it in his pocket. "I don't like doing this, Ray, because I know it hurts—but you give me no option."

Jerome saw that the doctor's blue eyes were again developing their inhuman, laser-like quality. He had time for one spasm of alarm. . . .

The pain was a flower unfolding in his brain with time-lapse rapidity. And with it there was knowledge, wordlessly received knowledge, interlaced with his own memories. The rigid Dorrinian ethic lays down that transfers may only be effected into the bodies of Terrans who are soon to die of incurable disease . . . Birkett was a cancer patient . . . the basic mind-matter interaction is control of the biological processes in one's own body . . . after a successful transfer a Dorrinian eradicates all the ailments he has inherited . . . family doctors are in a good position to select suitable target bodies, sometimes without their owners ever realizing they are seriously ill, as was the case with Arthur Starzynski . . . therefore key Dorrinians living on Earth are

81

*often small-town medics . . . the danger of a transfer failure is
ever present . . . it could lead to extensive loss of life if buildings
were set alight, something the Dorrinian ethic cannot countenance . . . the danger is obviated by introducing a Dorrinian-
developed chemical into the target's system . . . the chemical is
in turn absorbed by the target's clothing, making the garments
into heat barriers . . . inward reflection of the heat also ensures
complete destruction of the corpse, concealing the significant
factor of common illness . . . Pitman administered the chemical
in the form of cachous if the target was fond of candy . . . two
failed transfers in a row . . . bad sign . . . ominous . . . Prince
Belzor. . . .*

Jerome was abruptly returned to the world of blurry sunlight. Gasping, he forced his eyes to range in on Pitman,
shrinking him into sharp focus. Pitman was leaning forward
and staring intently at Jerome, but his eyes had lost their
mesmeric power. For the first time since Jerome had met him
he looked troubled, uncertain.

"Were you followed here, Ray?" he said.

"I don't believe . . . How would I know?"

"Think back over the journey," Pitman said urgently. "Did
you notice a . . .?" He stopped speaking, mouth down-curved
in shock, and pitched forward as an invisible *something* hit him
with an impact which made the entire boat shudder. An
instant later the sound of a gunshot rolled out across the lake,
drawing squawks of protest from birds.

Jerome let go of the oars and gripped the side of the boat,
which was wallowing in reaction to the crashing sprawl of
Pitman's body. He gaped at the doctor, at the back of his
jacket where a ragged hole pulsed crimson, and he struggled
to put the evidence together. The evidence said that somebody
on the shore of the lake had just shot Pitman with a rifle—but
the evidence had to be suspect because too many terrible and
unprecedented things had already occurred that day. Jerome
scanned the lakeside near his house, the area from which the
shot seemed to have come, but was unable to see anything out

of the ordinary. Feeling curiously numb, he slid down on to his knees, wondering how he would tend the fallen doctor, and in the instant of lowering his head he felt rather than heard a rushing in the air. It was a fluttery disturbance of the atmosphere, with a hint of power to it, quickly followed by the sound of another shot.

Jerome threw himself to the floor of the boat, appalled by the realization that the gunman—in defiance of all the laws of a formerly sane continuum—had also tried to kill him.

Pitman gave a burbling sigh and one of his hands groped towards Jerome. Spurred by irrational hope, Jerome squirmed a half-circle, keeping below the rowlocks, until he could look into Pitman's face. All notions about the doctor somehow being fit enough to use his unearthly powers to effect a miracle immediately fled Jerome's mind. Pitman's mouth was open, the teeth uniformly red, spanned by a swelling diaphragm of blood.

"You can't die," Jerome whispered. "This is all your fault."

Pitman's eyelids flickered and the crimson hymen ruptured into gory tatters on his chin. "Sorry . . . the Prince is . . . too. . . ." The barely audible words faded and were lost.

"Prince? *Prince?*" Jerome could hear his own voice rising to an hysterical whine. "I've nothing to do with any Prince. You've got to tell somebody that."

He grasped Pitman's shoulder, gave it a single shake and snatched his hand away, newly educated on the subject of death. There was no sound except for the patient lapping of small waves around the boat. Jerome rolled on to his back and stared into the sky as questions seethed in his mind. Did the person who had murdered Pitman positively want to kill him as well, or had the second shot merely been prompted by some gangsterish idea of doing a tidy job and silencing a witness? Was it likely that the assassin, believing the second shot had hit Jerome, had already fled? That one could be resolved quickly enough, by raising his head and peering over the side of the boat—but visualizing the possible consequences led him to the most important question of all. Was he going to get out of the situation alive?

The answer is NO!

Jerome flinched as the message impacted with his consciousness. There was a moment of fear and confusion—then came the knowledge that he was dealing with a second telepath. And with that knowledge was the understanding that the newcomer's personality was vastly different from that of Pitman. The doctor had been a mysterious and threatening figure, but he had also—and Jerome could appreciate it more in retrospect—projected regret for what he felt he had to do. That undercurrent of emotion had lent him a certain humanity, a quality which was totally lacking in the mental imprint of his slayer. During the brief psychic contact Jerome had sensed a chilling self-interest, an arrogance and amorality, an utter ruthlessness. There had also been the disturbing suggestion of a potency which far outweighed Pitman's, of an inhuman power which a superstitious person might describe as satanic.

As the word formed in Jerome's mind he caught a memory-glimpse of a pale face and a contemptuous smile, a pike-jawed smile which showed only the bottom teeth. The man he had encountered at the filling station! Jerome identified the second telepath, *knowing* himself to be correct, and in the same moment felt a new kind of darkness gather round him. He knew now that throughout the confrontation with Pitman his despair had never been absolute. There had always been that scintilla of hope, of belief that an oldster with a three-piece suit and a Santa Claus complexion could not actually pull the trigger—but the man from the filling station came into a different category altogether. With him there could be no reprieve.

That is CORRECT!

Again the communication sledged into Jerome with near-physical force, serving as a carrier for other patterns which impressed themselves directly upon his brain. He was compelled to view himself through the eyes of his adversary—weak, cowardly, contemptible, ignorant, insignificant. There was no hatred for Jerome in that other mind, for the simple reason that he was too unimportant. He was nothing more than a temporary inconvenience.

"Why waste time on me?" Jerome said aloud. The boat was more than a hundred metres from the shore and he knew his voice would not carry the distance, but the act of composing a sentence and speaking seemed a good way for a non-telepath to isolate and project a single thought. He braced himself for another intangible hammer blow, but there was no response from the man with the rifle.

"Look, I don't give a damn about what was going on between you and Pitman," he said. "All I want is to be allowed to go home. I can't harm you. Please let me go."

Again there was no response. Jerome stared into the impartial blue lens of the sky and tried to read the telepathic silence. One interpretation was that the pallid man had accepted the logic of his argument and had quietly departed the scene, but Jerome's instincts told him otherwise. There had been no reply because the killer on the shore saw no point in replying. He was still there, near the house, waiting for . . . What *was* he waiting for?

Jerome had hardly framed the question when the answer came to him. Rowing out to the centre of the lake with Pitman he had been heading into a breeze—and now that same breeze was gently taking the boat back towards its starting point. It would have been quite easy for a man with a hunting rifle to sink the rowboat and force Jerome into the water, but that would require a volley of shots and might attract attention. A much more efficient course was to be patient, to wait a few minutes until the target had helplessly drifted to the shore and despatch him with a single round. In the event, it would not even be necessary to fire the rifle, because the man from the filling station was capable of killing Jerome in a dozen different ways, all of them silent. . . .

So it isn't going to be my heart that does it, after all, Jerome thought in a kind of arctic bemusement as he lay on his back on the damp timbers of the boat. *Pitman's advice about a check-up was wasted . . . there isn't going to be time for my arteries to finish silting themselves up . . . I had to get in between people from another world who—God knows why—want to kill each other . . . and there's damn all I can do about it . . . because . . . because. . . .*

Jerome abruptly became aware of the shotgun. It was partially underneath Pitman's prone body and the stock was nudging painfully into his own back. Grunting with the effort, he turned himself over and—hampered by the need to keep below the side of the boat—worked the gun free of Pitman's dead weight. There was a comforting familiarity about its metalwork and oiled wood. It was no match for a rifle, but if he could keep the weapon hidden until the boat was close to the shore and then get in a quick shot its scattering effect would slightly reduce the odds against him.

Do you take me for a FOOL? The alien thought was loaded with contempt, reinforced by a vision of Jerome as something akin to a hairless baby rat, pink and squirming.

Jerome strove to fend off the intrusion. The shotgun was an old Stevens 12-gauge he had inherited from his father and he had only the vaguest ideas about its performance. He broke it open, with the intention of checking on whether Pitman had put in shells loaded with skeet shot or something with more carrying power, but there came yet another mental assault.

Do you really EXPECT me to ALLOW you to bring your TOY within range?

The baby rat was vivid in Jerome's mind now—a glistening blob of unformed protoplasm—and the heel of a boot was stamping down on it. Sickened, Jerome concentrated his gaze on the twin yellow-gleaming circles of the cartridge bases, knowing all the while that his adversary had too great an advantage. Even if he got as close as fifty metres the shotgun would be an annoyance rather than a real threat to a rifleman, and the latter's ability to divine exactly what Jerome was thinking and doing made the situation doubly hopeless. The only factor which might have given him a fighting chance would have been solid lead slugs in the shotgun, but he had never owned that kind of ammunition. . . .

If I can't fool a mind-reader, Jerome thought as he groped in his jacket for his pocket knife, *the least I can do is make things harder for him. Confuse the issue. Use double-think. But how do I do that? No good thinking about something totally irrelevant like an orange . . . only gives the game away . . . become an automaton . . . use reflexes instead of words or thought pictures . . . oh god one of the shells is jammed in the ejector . . . should have done something about that thing years ago . . . and insult the bastard let him know what you think of him . . . have to pry the shell out with my knife . . . hello you ugly bastard you're not just going to walk all over me you know . . . come out come OUT that's better. . . .*

Jerome threw the knife aside, closed up the shotgun and raised himself high enough to look over the side. He was about eighty metres from the shore and he could see the pallid man standing in the shade of a crack willow near the house. Not giving himself time to think, Jerome sat up higher, put the gun to his shoulder and took aim.

Go ahead! The derisive challenge washed over Jerome. *Waste your birdshot!*

"Hello, you ugly bastard," Jerome said aloud, desperately trying to hold the foresight on his target. The slight movement of the boat was making the task difficult, and seconds were slipping by, and no amount of effort on his part could shut out of his mind a memory-image of his knife cutting through the tube of the shell in the right-hand chamber, leaving only a single strand of plastic. The barrage of scorn which was clubbing at his mind became tinged with alarm and the figure on the shore made a sudden movement.

Jerome squeezed off his shot and allowed the recoil to topple him backwards into the boat.

He crouched beside Pitman's body, ears ringing with manufactured thunder, and tried to *feel* what was happening at the edge of the lake. He had no doubt that the hundreds of lead pellets massed as a single projectile, still held together by the severed tube of the cartridge, would have been able to carry the distance to the shore and deliver a devastating punch—*but had his aim been good enough?* Shotgun sights were not designed for that kind of aiming, the boat had been rocking, and he had been in a state of panic. The psychic pressure from the rifleman appeared to have ceased, but that could mean he had decided to lie low and await his chance to end the strange duel.

Jerome weighed the possibilities and reluctantly came to the conclusion that he had nothing to gain by allowing himself to go on drifting towards the shore. If the pallid man had not been put out of action it would be better to find out sooner than later. Jerome gave an unhappy sigh and raised his head, wondering if a person who received a high-velocity bullet between the eyes had time to feel pain or realize what had happened to him.

There was no movement on the shore, nothing out of the ordinary to see. The afternoon sun glowed placidly on the walls of his house, visual echo of a hundred mellow weekends. Jerome studied the area of shade beneath the willow, but the various patches of colour he could distinguish remained ambiguous. He looked around for the oars he had released, found them floating within reach and manoeuvred them up into the rowlocks. In order to row properly he had to slide his feet under Pitman's body, but the lolling pressure was merely something else to be accepted in a day which was testing his endurance to the limit.

As he pulled towards the side of the lake he imagined a rifle target stitched to his back and visualized it as seen through a sighting scope, growing larger with each second. So clear did the mental picture become that he was forced to wonder if it could be yet another telepathic transmission, a teasing punishment for his act of defiance, and with the accompanying spasm of alarm the tightness returned to his chest. He slackened off his pace, imposed a slow regularity on his breathing and practised the new art of tolerating the intolerable until the boat was nuzzling into reeds and mud. The water reached up to his knees in clamming intimacy as he stepped out.

He picked up the shotgun, got his finger around the second trigger and waded the last few paces on to dry land. The first thing he saw was a hunting rifle lying at the base of the willow tree. On the far side of the tree was visible a khaki-clad shoulder and arm, and Jerome realized that the man from the filling station was sitting with his back to the trunk, facing away from him and the lake. What he could see of the man was perfectly motionless, but the exposed hand was very close to the rifle.

Jerome considered the idea that he was being toyed with, lured into a trap, and was able to dismiss it. The personality with whom he had been in telepathic contact had been far too cold and inhuman to countenance any kind of indirection. Had he been in a position to kill Jerome during the last few minutes Jerome would be dead—it was as simple as that—but perhaps he was only lightly unconscious. Easing his feet out of his waterlogged shoes, Jerome approached the tree in silence. He stooped and gripped the rifle by its muzzle and flung the weapon aside. The exposed hand did not move.

Paradoxically more anxious than before, Jerome circled to the other side of the tree, keeping the shotgun at the ready, and halted as he got his first direct look at the seated figure. The man from the filling station had taken the 12-gauge shell on the right cheekbone. That side of his face was caved in and at the centre of the bloody depression was visible the bright orange plastic of the cartridge tube, barely projecting from the ruptured tissue. His head was in an upright position, tilted back against the tree for support. His right eye was ruined, hidden by pulverized flesh and skin, but the left one was open. He was still alive, in spite of the dreadful wound, and the single eye was staring at Jerome with a kind of serene malevolence.

Jerome backed away, shaking his head, and turned to flee—but he was too late.

The light seemed to appear *inside* his skull, whiting out his surroundings, whiting out his consciousness, then he was falling through the whiteness into an ocean of white radiance.

Chapter 5

There was something strange about the three men and two women who were regarding Jerome so anxiously.

It was not the shoulder-length hair of the men, although that was a style he had not seen since around 1990; nor was it the dress of all five, although that in itself was highly unusual. They were wearing short blue-grey skirts which looked like silk, and loose upper garments of a similar material which was cut into narrow strips and appended from black collars. The only differentiation for sex was that the men's collars were chokers, while those of the women sat lower and were cut square.

Beyond the group Jerome could see part of a circular, windowless room with a domed ceiling, and that too had an indefinable strangeness which was nothing to do with the architecture. He sat quite still, aware of the pressure of soft upholstery against his body, and tried to isolate and identify the unfamiliar element which was common to everything in his surroundings.

The tallest of the three men shook his head and said, "Na tostin arvo kald." The woman beside him gasped, covered her face with her hands and turned away.

Jerome watched her in a kind of numb bemusement and far down in his consciousness, like a prisoner awakening in a dungeon, a sly uneasiness began to stir. Perhaps, instead of pursuing the elusive subtlety in the environment, he should be asking himself where he was and who these. . . .

I've got it! The discovery filled him with dull wonderment. *I'm not wearing my glasses—but I can see perfectly. It's all hard-edged and detailed . . . near and far . . . I'm in a hospital and they've done something to my eyes!*

He felt a momentary satisfaction before the uneasiness returned amid a swirl of questions.

Exactly where am I? Did the man from the filling station shoot me? If this is a hospital, why aren't the staff properly dressed? And why is it that I don't really give a damn about any of this?

The tall man moved closer to Jerome, leaned over him and said, "My name is Pirt Sull Conforden. Are you Raymond Jerome?"

"My first name is Rayner," Jerome replied, wondering at the odd timbre of his own voice. "It's a family name."

"Very well, Rayner. There are many things you will want to know and are entitled to know, so you and I are going to talk for a while." Conforden glanced at his companions and they immediately turned and walked away, one of the men putting an arm around the woman who appeared to be in distress. They went through an archway and moved out of Jerome's view in a narrow corridor which seemed to have curving walls like those of a tunnel. Jerome began to wonder if he was in some kind of an underground complex, but the curious apathy he was experiencing prevented him from pursuing the matter.

"Why is that woman upset?" he said, again noticing an unusual quality in his voice.

"A close friend has just died. You will understand later." Conforden's English was unaccented but spoken with a precision which suggested he was a good linguist using a slightly unfamiliar tongue. He appeared to be in his late thirties and had an oval face which was boyish and at the same time stamped with a look of world-weariness. His skin was pale and so uniformly flawless that it could have been sprayed with matt plastic.

"I know you are feeling muzzy and detached," Conforden said, "and there will probably be some nausea, for which I apologize in advance. Those are the effects of drugs in your system and they will be short-lived."

"Drugs? Anaesthetics? My eyes. . . ."

"Don't worry about your eyes. Is your vision better or worse than before?"

"Much better," Jerome said. "Is this a trauma unit? Have I been shot?"

Conforden shook his head and spoke with a persuasive gentleness. "You are in perfect health. I want you to relax. Allow yourself to float, but try to absorb the information I am going to give you. Much of it will be difficult to assimilate in the beginning, but I am here to answer all your questions, and I can assure you that you will come to no harm in this new phase of your existence."

Jerome considered the other man's final words, dreamily aware that he should have found them ominous. "That sounded like a welcome to heaven or hell or some place in between."

"No, you are still very much alive," Conforden replied. "It was a welcome to the planet you know as Mercury."

Jerome stared into the dome of the ceiling for what might have been one minute or five. His brain had been turned into a ball of cotton, a pliant mass which was unable to respond properly to any kind of stimulus. He could feel the objects which were his heart and lungs going about their customary business, but they were as remote as pulsars, lost in druggy distance.

All right, the proposition is that I'm on Mercury, he thought. *Shouldn't be too hard to deal with that one.*

He drew his lips into a smile. "Are you going to tell me how I got here?"

"It is essential that you be told everything."

"Just tell me how I got to Mercury."

Conforden frowned, detecting the verbal challenge, but his voice lost none of its softness. "First, it is necessary for you to understand that Nitha Roll Movik—the Dorrinian you knew as Pitman—never had any intention of killing you. We are an ethical people who do not countenance the taking of life."

Jerome recalled the events at the lake, leached-out images on a fuzzy screen. "The gun."

"That was merely a physical restraint. Others before you have accidentally learned too much about Dorrinian operations on Earth, forcing us to silence them. The method we use is the transference of the personality of a Dorrinian volunteer into the body of the Terran. But, even for a super-telepath, it is difficult to focus a kald lens on one individual at interplanetary distances. Normally it takes several hours, but the process can be compressed into one hour or less if the target kald is immobile in an unpopulated area of Earth. *That* is why Movik held you so long at gunpoint—he was waiting for the transference to be effected.

"Unfortunately, he waited too long."

"When you are ready I want you to tell me exactly what happened to him."

"Don't you know?" Jerome said, feeling that he was somehow straying away from a vastly more important point. "Can't you read my mind?"

"Not really. My telepathic faculties are not very well developed. There is something about another firearm . . . a duel. . . ."

"We were out on the lake in my rowboat," Jerome said, still locked in an unnatural calmness while the silent clamour echoed through lower levels of his mind. "A man at the side of the lake shot Pitman with a rifle. He tried to kill me as well, but I . . . I managed to bring him down."

An unreadable expression appeared on Conforden's face. "What did this man look like?"

"Ugly. Mean." Jerome visualized the pallid face, the pike-mouthed smile. "I couldn't look him straight in the eye."

"It was the Prince himself," Conforden said slowly. "You were lucky to get away with your life."

"That's the impression I. . . ." Jerome paused as sluggish connections were finally completed in his mind. "How did I get away? I tried to talk all this out with Pitman. I told him this transference business was no different than murder in my eyes, but he didn't have time to answer me."

94

"It is a reciprocal process," Conforden said. "When a transfer is completed the Terran and the Dorrinian exchange bodies."

"I should have guessed," Jerome said resignedly, and when he raised his hands he saw at once that they belonged to a stranger.

Chapter 6

The period of adjustment was uneven.

There were times when all Jerome could do was gaze into a mirror and make random movements with his head and limbs. Occasionally the movements would be rapid and unpremeditated, as though the image in the glass might be tricked into making a slow response and thus betray an elaborate practical joke.

His new face stared back at him all the while, preoccupied and solemn. It was a comparatively youthful face, more square of chin than the one he had always known, and with a black stubble of beard which contrasted with his former sparseness of facial hair. The features were regular, if unremarkable, and had he been able to think in such terms he would have felt he had done quite well out of the exchange. It was, he sensed, the kind of face which would have found favour with Anne Kruger—but she was part of another existence and her sexual preferences were now a matter of complete indifference to him.

As the drugs migrated from his system he experienced mood swings, alternating between outrage and passive acceptance of all that had happened. And between spells of drowsiness he tried to recall and assimilate his first long interview with Pirt Sull Conforden. With hindsight he understood that his confrontation with the man from the filling station—the man referred to by the Dorrinians as Prince Belzor—had involved an unseen third party. It had also been even more dangerous than he had realized at the time.

The body Jerome now inhabited had belonged to a Dorrinian super-telepath called Orkra Rell Blamene, who had volunteered to make the transfer which was necessary to silence Jerome. It appeared that the Dorrinians on Mercury had been aware that Pitman was in trouble, but had been left ignorant of the circumstances because of the difficulty of mental communication over interplanetary distances. Mortally wounded, rapidly approaching dissolution, Pitman had been unable to send any kind of warning about what had happened to him. And as a result Blamene had arrived on Earth, had assumed Jerome's physical form, just in time to be overwhelmed by the awesome powers of the Prince.

"Are you quite certain that's what happened?" Jerome had asked, while still lost in a chemical fog. "The man I shot looked like he was dying."

"That particular body was dying, but Prince Belzor cannot be killed so easily," Conforden had replied. "We know that Blamene survived the transfer by less than a minute. He would have been extremely vulnerable at that point, and it is almost certain that the Prince, needing a new incarnation, simply displaced him."

Later, with the partial return of acuity, Jerome had brooded on the new levels of meaning invested for him in the term "displaced". The mundane word now had dark associations. It conjured up visions of the bizarre scene at Parson's Lake . . . the alien superman slumped against a tree, incapacitated and hideously wounded . . . requiring a fresh vehicle for his inhuman personality . . . fixing that single remaining eye, that evil eye (*the evil eye!*) upon the fleeing figure of Jerome/ Blamene . . . effortlessly and mercilessly compelling that figure to halt, to stand still, to submit to . . . *displacement.*

Having admitted the reality of displacement, Jerome was forced to go further and acknowledge the disquieting idea that his own familiar body now housed an alien being. Millions of kilometres away, back on Earth, there was a man who appeared to be Rayner Jerome, who was possibly living in Rayner Jerome's house, who was accepted by Rayner Jerome's colleagues—but who was in fact an interloper from another world. The thought was intensely distasteful to Jerome, filling him with helpless resentment. His body had been a troublesome organic machine, marred by faults and threatening the final breakdown, but it had been *his*. Displacement was a supremely unnatural event, and Jerome did not have the emotional repertoire to deal with it and all its implications, but he knew that nobody should ever have been violated the way he had been violated. The deed had a sulphurous tang of evil about it, one which was intensified in his drug-shadowed mind by the mystery which surrounded the Dorrinians.

In spite of all he had garnered from Pitman and Conforden, when it came to understanding their racial motivations he felt rather like an ancient Greek pondering on the meaning of lightning flashes over Mount Olympus. The Dorrinians had God-like powers, that much was certain, but was there something genuinely Manichean in the battle they were conducting on Earth? Jerome believed he had rid himself of all traces of religious conviction, and yet his fuddled consciousness insisted on building fantasy edifices out of puns, quasi-facts and wild associations, many of them connected with the satanic figure of the man from the filling station—Prince . . . Prince of Darkness . . . Belzor . . . Beelzebub . . . helios . . . heliac . . . Hell. . . .

He had been told that the surreptitious invasion of Earth, the invasion of privacy, had been going on for more than three millennia. What was the point of it all?

Was it possible that occasional rents in the Dorrinian veil of secrecy had linked them to the terrible spectacle of the fire death and had been the genesis of certain elements in Terran mythologies and religions?

And why were the other members of the Dorrinian race engaged in a deadly struggle with the Prince?

Too many questions, Jerome told himself as the drifts of sleep gathered in his brain. *Too much to think about. . . .*

* * *

"Come on, lad—you can't lie in your pit for ever!"

The man whose words had aroused Jerome had the button eyes, wide mouth and protruding circular ears of a storybook gnome, but the most remarkable things about him, as far as Jerome was concerned, were his short hair and Earth-style shirt and slacks. Still not properly awake, Jerome allowed himself to be deceived by the irrational hope that he had escaped from a protracted and vivid nightmare. He sat upright on the couch, eagerly, then realized he was in the same circular room as before, a chamber carved into the rock strata of Mercury. The clarity of his unaided vision was confirmation enough.

"Name's Joe Thwaite," the stranger said. "Spinster of this parish for the last eleven years, but before that resident in the beautiful township of Barrow-in-Furness."

"Barrow-in-Furness?" Jerome began to feel lost. "Isn't that in England?"

"Certainly is. Best town in the whole ruddy country."

Jerome was still adrift between two worlds. "But you don't have an English accent."

"And you don't have an American one. Not any more." Thwaite produced a gnomish grin. "Accents are mainly a matter of muscle development, and you've got Dorrinian speech centres now, so you speak with a good Dorrinian twang—just like everybody else around here."

"I . . . I don't understand."

Thwaite peered closely into Jerome's face. "You must have been drugged to the eyeballs, lad. Don't you remember anything of what Pirt told you about the colony?"

"The colony? It's all so. . . ."

"Look, the main thing to remember is that transfers work both ways," Thwaite said. "We've got more than a hundred Terrans here. Everybody the Dorrinians swapped places with in the last few decades—even the ones who burned up."

Jerome struggled to encompass what the other man was saying. It had been explained to him that each personality transfer was a reciprocal event, but he had been too stupefied to take the thought to its logical conclusion.

He was not the only one of his kind on Mercury.

There *had* to be a colony of reluctant exiles—men and women who had shared the devastating experience of losing consciousness on Earth and awakening on a distant planet. According to Thwaite, even those individuals who had attracted the public's interest by "dying" of spontaneous combustion were members of the colony—in which case he could actually dredge many of his fellow exiles' names out of his memory.

Jerome felt a coolness on his spine as he considered the idea. His capacity for wonder had been overloaded by the events of the recent past, but there was a singular and disquieting strangeness in the thought of walking into a room and being introduced to a series of people whose names he associated with the horrific photographs in the *Examiner*'s files. How was he supposed to relate to a man or woman who had first registered on his consciousness as an image of a mound of ash terminating in a pair of slippered feet? And that was not to be the worst of his tribulations. . . .

"Is there somebody called Sammy?" he said warily. "Sammy Birkett?"

"Yes, he was brought in just a few hours before . . ." Thwaite broke off, his narrow brow contracting. "How did you know?"

"I was there when the transfer went wrong. I saw him . . . his body . . . burn up."

"You mean you were actually *there!*" The black cabochons of Thwaite's eyes glinted with malicious pleasure. "That sort of thing isn't supposed to happen. Belzor must have got them buggers running around in the proverbial ever-decreasing circles. Come on, lad—on your feet! The others have got to hear about this." Thwaite picked up a small draw-neck bag which had been lying beside the couch and produced from it a shirt, slacks and underwear which he handed to Jerome. Although the garments bore no labels they were of commercial quality and could have passed as being made on Earth.

100

"Where am I supposed to go?" Jerome said.

"You'll soon get clued in. For starters, this bag contains all your worldly goods—which means a spare set of clothes and a toothbrush," Thwaite said. "The Dorries supply you with that much free of charge. They say it's out of the goodness of their hearts. Don't you believe it! The Marks and Sparks look is supposed to help us feel more at ease, but it's actually to set us apart and make us easy to keep an eye on. Same with our hair. When you see anybody who isn't done up like an Armenian poofter you know he's a transplant from Earth."

"Thanks for telling me," Jerome said, deriving some slight comfort from identification of a familiar character-type. Thwaite's homely presence made Mercury appreciably less alien. Jerome stood up, put on the proffered underpants and winced as the rayon-like material came in contact with his groin.

"That's something else they give us for nothing," Thwaite commented. "Free vasectomies. When a super-tele comes near his transfer time he gets snipped. Prevents the Terrans from producing hybrids."

"Hybrids?"

"Maybe that isn't the right word, but you know what I mean. Would the offspring of two Terries in Dorrie bodies be classified as Terries or Dorries?"

"Good question," Jerome said, finding unexpected difficulty in dealing with a shirt button.

"Damn right it's a good question!" Thwaite tugged thoughtfully at one of his protuberant ears. "Have to give the Dorries their due, though—they could have de-balled us instead. Know something, lad? I'd been finished with the old how's-your-father for five or six years when I got transferred. Sixty-six I was. There I was . . . sat there in The Globe in Ulverston, downing a pint of Hartley's best . . . Used to take the bus through to Ulverston every Thursday, 'cause it's market day and the pubs stay open right through. . . . Next

101

thing I knew I was awakening up in this very room . . . just where you are now. . . ."

Jerome looked up, momentarily abandoning the attempt to button his shirt. "A shock to the system."

Thwaite's lips developed a wry quirk. "You never spoke a truer word, lad. I'm used to most things around here after eleven years, but I can't get used to doing without my beer. You know, I sometimes think they could keep all their free love if I could just have a few pints of Hartley's best every now and then."

"Can't you brew your own beer?"

"The Dorries don't go in for alcohol, and the air in this place is so well scrubbed there aren't any wild yeasts."

"There's something wrong with the buttons on this shirt," Jerome said.

"It's your Dorrie fingers that's wrong—they've never dealt with buttons before."

"But surely I can exercise full control over them."

"Think so? Just wait till you try using a knife and fork. It'll be a week before you can eat your dinner properly." Thwaite came closer and efficiently buttoned Jerome's shirt. "You'll have to manage the trousers yourself, lad—nobody's going to start rumours about me being a poofter."

"I should hope not." Jerome remained silent for a moment as he concentrated on the task of clothing his younger, slimmer body, then the sheer abnormality of his circumstances overwhelmed him once more, like tidal waters that had been only temporarily checked. "I keep expecting to find it's all a dream."

"It's no dream, lad. You're on the planet Mercury and, from what Pirt told me, you had some advance knowledge of the set-up to cushion the shock for you. Others weren't so lucky."

"All right," Jerome said. "Exactly where am I on Mercury?"

"At the north pole. About sixty feet down."

102

Jerome had to convert the distance to metric units before he could think about it. "Is that all? What about the heat from the Sun?"

"There isn't much heat at the poles," Thwaite said. "The Dorries are always moaning about how unlucky they were, but—if you swallow their mythology about the big comet—they got off pretty light."

"Mythology? Pirt said it was history."

Thwaite shrugged. "In that case they were bloody lucky to end up with zero axial tilt. Their twilight zone disappeared, but at least they were left with a static twilight spot at each pole. If Mercury's axis had tilted the twilight spots would be roaming around in circles and none of us would be here."

"You sound pretty sceptical," Jerome said as he succeeded in overcoming his last button.

"It's the way I was brought up, lad. Mercury also has what they call spin-orbit resonance, with one of its days being exactly equal to two of its years. I daresay it's possible that the comet gave it an axial spin very close to the right value, and tidal friction with the Sun made the final adjustments—but I have a feeling that would take more than a few thousand years."

"Were you a professional astronomer?"

"In *Barrow?*" Thwaite snorted his amusement. "No, I'm just a keen amateur. Being transported to another world in mid-pint gives you an interest in these things, if you know what I mean. Are you ready to go?"

"I'm not sure."

"The sooner you get out and mingle with the others the better you'll feel," Thwaite said. "It's amazing how quickly you adapt. Look at me—I even got used to having a face like one of the Seven Dwarves. Let's go."

"Very well." Jerome felt timid and apprehensive, but he forced himself to keep abreast of Thwaite as they left the circular chamber and turned left into a long corridor which

103

was illuminated by white globes attached to the ceiling. He judged himself to be slightly taller than in his previous incarnation and suddenly was very much aware of the mechanics of walking. His body was an ungainly and precariously balanced structure, the proper control of which demanded more skill and strength than he seemed to possess. After only a few paces he began steadying himself by touching the curving wall.

"Don't worry about the weakness," Thwaite said. "Superteles don't eat or drink for two or three days before a transfer shot. Once you get a couple of steaks down your neck you'll be as right as rain."

The realization that he was hungry turned Jerome's thoughts towards the problems of food supply in a totally hostile environment. "Where does the steak come from?"

"They grow them like giant mushrooms and keep slicing bits off. The Dorries are good at that kind of thing. They'll never do a decent Cumberland sausage, though."

Thwaite began to reminisce about the various items of British food and drink he missed most, but Jerome was distracted by the sight of other men and women walking in the corridor. Most were dressed in Earth-style clothing, but a few had the ribbon-blouses and skirts which proclaimed them to be Dorrinians. Almost without exception the people were tall and slimly built, and Jerome decided it was an effect of the lesser gravity of Mercury. He felt no lighter than he had ever done, but that had to be because his inherited body was accustomed to the conditions. A number of the Terrans gave Jerome amiable nods and murmured welcomes, but it was only after he had received a particularly warm smile from a young brunette that he realized he was drawing much more attention from the women than from the men.

"You're going to be all right here, lad," Thwaite said, glancing back appreciatively at the brunette. "That's Donna Sinclair. She had her eye on Blamene for a couple of years, but he was too wrapped up in a Dorrie woman to pay her any heed. Now that you've stepped into his shoes, so to speak, you'll be able to play substitute—you lucky bugger."

Jerome was unable to think about what had become trivia. "Did you say lucky?"

"I did. I don't know what you were like back in the USA, but now you're a fine-looking. . . ."

"Where are we going?" Jerome cut in, noticing that the corridor had widened into the semblance of a busy underground street. "What is this place?"

"You're near the centre of the Precinct," Thwaite said. "The Terrans all live and work within a couple of hundred yards of here. This is our territory. Any Dorries you see are mostly super-telepaths getting used to Earth languages and customs. If you're lucky you might land a teaching job."

"Does everybody work?"

"There's no serious compulsion, but most people would rather have something to do. If anybody absolutely refuses to work we just leave them to themselves and let them stew. In the end they generally decide they'd like to join in. The only ones who stay apart permanently are the old-time-religion types who refuse to believe they haven't died, but they're very rare birds these days and we don't mind carrying them. They wouldn't be much use, anyroad. You can't get much work out of some silly sod who's convinced he's in Purgatory."

"It's not hard to see how they get that idea," Jerome said, scanning his surroundings. The floor, walls and ceiling of the tunnel-corridor were of a uniform grey and there was a quality of sterile cheerlessness to the light emitted by the overhead globes. The thought of having to spend the rest of his life in such an environment inspired him with a mixture of sadness, claustrophobia and despair.

"It's not so bad here," Thwaite replied. "You'll get used to it."

"Think so?"

"You haven't much choice." Thwaite halted at an unmarked doorway, one of many in the curving walls. "You go in here for your placement interview. There's nothing much to it. You talk to a panel of three and they work out how you can best be fitted into the community. I'm one of the three, because I'm the equivalent of the town clerk for the Precinct. The others are Mel Zednik, our Mayor, and Pirt Conforden, who's the Dorrinian Director responsible for Terran affairs. He's the one who was talking to you in the recovery room while you were still groggy, and he's a decent enough bloke—for a Dorrie, that is."

Jerome studied his companion's face. "Why do I get the impression you're praising him with faint damns?"

"Couldn't tell you, lad." Thwaite's dark eyes twinkled, qualifying his protest. "They tell me I was about to peg out, back there in Barrow in '85, so I've had eleven extra years and a lot more to come. Nobody in his right mind could complain about a bargain like that. Could they?"

"What if you'd only been fifty and had nothing much wrong with you?"

"Expediency transfers like yours are rare."

"That doesn't alter the facts of my case."

"You should talk to Pirt about it," Thwaite said, giving an exaggerated flourish which invited Jerome to precede him into the room. "I'm sure he'll be most sympathetic."

Doubtful about the other man's sincerity, Jerome entered a small room which was uncomfortably warm and stuffy. The furniture consisted of four simple chairs equally spaced at a circular table. Already seated were the Dorrinian with whom Jerome had first conversed and a grey-blond man in Terran dress. The latter, who had to be Zednik, had bushy eyebrows and a deeply lined face, and he might have been very old, although his body was slim and held upright with evident lack of effort. Jerome was reminded that the Mercurian gravity was much less inimical than Earth's. Thwaite brusquely performed unnecessary introductions, took a seat and invited Jerome to do likewise. Jerome considered refusing, then decided it would be a stereotyped reaction. He sat down, fixed his gaze on the Dorrinian—who was directly opposite—and waited, his face carefully impassive.

Conforden gave him a wry smile. "Well, Rayner, one doesn't need to be a telepath to tell that you are not happy here on Dorrin."

"Does that surprise you?" Jerome refused to return the smile. "Why should I be anything other than outraged?"

"We saved your life."

"From one of your own kind. I'm not impressed."

"It doesn't matter whether you're impressed or not," Zednik put in, speaking with the kind of mildness often used by those who enjoy the exercise of authority. "The fact is that you're here and you'll just have to adapt—like everybody else."

"No, Rayner made a legitimate point," Conforden said. "The circumstances of his transfer were far from normal, and I—on behalf of the people of Dorrin—have to apologize. Prince Belzor is a renegade and has been disowned by all Dorrinians, but we still have a certain amount of responsibility for his actions."

"And that's another thing! I'm sick of all this gobbledegook, all the verbal white noise." Jerome could hear his voice rising, but he felt no obligation to keep himself in check. "What the hell is going on here? You sit around and condemn this Belzor character, but what right have any of you to interfere with people's lives on Earth? Who told you you could butt in?"

"We're not alien beings," Conforden said quietly. "You can see that for yourself. We're from common stock. Nobody can say why our joint ancestors chose to put a colony on a world as uninhabitable as Dorrin. Perhaps in the beginning it was only a scientific research team—it was all too long ago for the evidence to have survived—but they did it. The peoples of Earth and Dorrin are brothers, and are mutually obligated to each other."

Jerome sighed. "Perhaps I'm still under the influence of your drugs, but was that meant to be an explanation of why Belzor is roaming around my world murdering people?"

"I think you should show a little more respect," Zednik said to Jerome, his tones no longer light. "You'll have to learn to. . . ."

Conforden silenced him by raising a hand. "It's all right, Mel—Rayner has been under a great deal of stress." He returned his attention to Jerome. "You know that Dorrinians are bound by a very strict code of ethics?"

"That's what Pitman kept telling me."

"After a successful transfer takes place the Dorrinian improves the health of the Terran body by direct mental control of its biological processes. That is a simple procedure for us, and it allows the Dorrinian to get many useful years out of the body. Physical ageing has to continue, however, and inevitably there comes a time when the Terran body weakens and begins to die. At that stage, with the resources of our mind science available to him, and working at close range, the Dorrinian could easily force a transfer with another Terran who was young and healthy. The temptation must be considerable. Any Dorrinian who transfers to Earth has effective immortality within his grasp—but our ethic forbids any further transfers. The Dorrinian always dies with the host body."

"Not always," Jerome said, almost to himself, as a curtain rolled back in his mind.

"As you say." Conforden sounded like a man who had been personally shamed. "Prince Belzor has been living on Earth for more than two thousand of your years. He has committed many crimes against your people."

Jerome was silent for a moment. "I was afraid of him."

"You had every right to be. Over the centuries the Prince has developed his powers to an unprecedented level. Even the strongest Dorrinians dare not go against him alone."

"In that case the smart thing would be to stay out of his way."

Conforden lowered his gaze. "That is what we have always done. It was a cowardly policy, and a mistaken one, because in the beginning the Prince could have been quickly overcome by a determined effort on our part. But we were few in number and there was always so much work to be done. It was always easier to let the Prince go his own way . . . unmolested . . . through all his successive incarnations. . . .

"And now, to use one of your Terran metaphors, the chickens are coming home to roost. The Prince has begun seeking us out."

"Why?" Jerome sensed he was nearing the edge of yet another conceptual precipice. "Why does he do that?"

Conforden raised his head, and his eyes locked with Jerome's. "Because he fears his reign is coming to an end. When we arrive on Earth in force, thousands of us in a single migration, the Prince will be required to answer for all his crimes."

The silence which descended on the room lasted perhaps twenty seconds, but for Jerome it seemed to go on a long time. He became aware of the muted breathing of the air supply system.

"May I presume," he said, holding his voice steady, "that you're going to expand on that?"

Conforden nodded. "We have no secrets here, Rayner. I can tell you that shortly before the Days of the Comet our ancestors had realized that extreme measures would be necessary to preserve the vital core of the Dorrinian culture. It was apparent that a huge proportion of the race was about to perish; therefore the ancients assembled four thousand of their most gifted individuals and devised a survival plan. The kalds of the Four Thousand were translated into an imperishable crystal matrix.

"I am a Dorrinian, but even I cannot fully comprehend the mind-matter interactions that were involved, so I can guess how difficult this concept must be for you. Telepathy is partly a physical process, involving the mental apportation of energies. Perhaps you can accept that if a personality can be impressed upon the molecular structure of a target brain, it can also be impressed on any other suitably complex structure. Let us say, for simplicity's sake, that the kald of each of the Four Thousand was transmogrified to become a unique giant molecule.

"It was, of course, necessary for the Four Thousand to abandon their biological forms in the process—but they did not die. On the contrary, their kalds have been safely preserved for more than three millennia and are merely awaiting reincarnation."

Conforden paused and looked solemnly at Jerome. "Are you with me thus far?"

"I think I may be moving ahead of you," Jerome replied. The excessive heat of the room was unable to combat the coldness which had been growing in him since he had made the intuitive leap and had begun to understand why, since Biblical times, strangers had walked in secret amid the peoples of Earth.

"Possibly you are, but I'm obliged to make the historical facts clear to you," Conforden said. "The Dorrinian word for the repository of the kalds of the Four Thousand is Thabbren, and that is how I shall refer to it. No Terran word could come near to expressing what the Thabbren means to Dorrinians. It is numinous beyond words, the ultimate sacred object, the soul of our race, the embodiment of our past and future. Any Dorrinian would unhesitatingly give his life to protect it—indeed the greatest honour to which a member of my race can aspire is that of becoming a Guardian. That is how we refer to them, simply as Guardians, because all else in our existence is subordinate to their single task."

"Are you a Guardian?" Jerome said.

"I have that honour."

"But there's more to the job than just keeping guard over the Thabbren, isn't there?" Jerome glanced at the other Terrans as he spoke. "There wouldn't be much point in preserving it for ever in this petrified warren. Correct?"

"Perfectly correct," Conforden said. "The Guardians were

110

charged with the additional responsibility of getting the Thabbren to Earth."

"Quite a responsibility."

"As you say." Conforden seemed unaware of the irony Jerome had employed. "Our lack of resources made it impossible for us to develop our own means of transporting the Thabbren across space. Instead, we began working undercover on Earth, placing Dorrinians in key positions, at first guiding Earth's racial consciousness towards astronomy and the idea of exploring space, then helping steer your science and technology in the appropriate direction. We were working towards one all-important event—the dispatch of a manned ship to Mercury."

Jerome sat up straighter. "You're not talking about the *Quicksilver*, are you? The ship that's already on its way?"

"I am," Conforden said. "One of the crew is a Dorrinian, one of a number we have placed in astronaut training programmes. His assignment is to pick up the Thabbren at a prearranged point on the surface."

"But how will you know where. . . .?" Jerome paused, his thoughts racing. "So there *isn't* any crashed ship from Outside?"

"Correct again, Rayner. We built a metal structure which looks as though it could be part of the hull of a large spacecraft, placed it on the surface and ensured that Earth would discover it. Eighteen Dorrinians lost their lives in that operation, but they understood the risks and we do not begrudge the sacrifice."

Jerome's eidetic memory was suddenly galvanized, producing an image of a semi-circular stamp on a discarded envelope. "When I was in Pitman's office back in Whiteford I noticed some mail for him from CryoCare. . . ."

"Movik was right when he decided that you should be transferred," Conforden said. "Yes, CryoCare is largely a Dorrinian enterprise."

"And do you have the four thousand bodies?"

111

"We do. It was a major task—finding that number of people who had no relations to complicate the issue, and who were dying of diseases we knew we could eliminate after the reincarnations. The need for total secrecy made things even more difficult, but we succeeded."

"Secrecy has always been a big thing with you people," Jerome said, voicing a minor criticism as a camouflage for the deep revulsion the Dorrinian's words had inspired in him. The calmly enunciated sentences were predicated on scenes of purest horror.

Conforden shook his head. "It doesn't come naturally to us. We have been forced to work in secret because of certain prejudices which are prevalent on Earth."

"Against body-snatching!"

"Your words prove my point, Rayner. Just think how much more extreme your reaction would have been had you lived in more ignorant and more superstitious times. The connection with human combustion alone would have been enough to brand all Dorrinians as emissaries of the Devil. As things are, we already have too many obstacles and dangers to face."

"Space flight itself is risky," Jerome said. "With the . . . ah . . . Thabbren being so important to you, is it wise to try getting it to Earth on what is, after all, a fairly primitive kind of ship? Shouldn't you hang on another fifty or hundred years until space travel is routine and safe?"

"That point has received a great deal of discussion." Conforden's eyes had a sad candour. "You have been away from your world for only three days. Have you already forgotten how things were? Do you really feel that Earth is entering the kind of period of enlightenment and stability which is necessary for interplanetary development?"

"It's hard to. . . ."

"Don't delude yourself, Rayner. As things are, the *Quicksilver* may well be the last ship Earth will send into space. Even if another civilization succeeds the present one, it could take tens of centuries for it to develop a space technology. We

112

Dorrinians have the patience to wait that long—after all, time no longer exists for the Four Thousand—but we do not have the resources. No, my friend, the Thabbren goes to Earth on the *Quicksilver*."

"Out of the solar frying pan into the nuclear fire?"

"That aspect of the situation has also been debated," Conforden said, speaking with his wordy precision. "We are confident of our ability to inject positive new elements into the Terran culture and reverse its downward trend. An overt Dorrinian presence on Earth will have tremendous potential for good. Indeed, that is one of the prime moral justifications for our involvement with your world."

"You're a highly ethical people," Jerome commented drily.

"As you say." Conforden's gaze hunted over Jerome's face. "Now, Rayner, you are more-or-less in possession of the full facts. The purpose of these placement interviews is to ascertain how each new arrival can best be fitted into the society of the Precinct, to optimize his contribution—but first we want your promise of co-operation. We want willing workers."

"I've been through this bit already, with Pitman," Jerome said. "And I told him I didn't like the idea of betraying everybody on Earth. I don't like what you've done to me personally—and I'm not going to work for you."

"That's not the way of it, lad," Thwaite put in, speaking for the first time since the start of the meeting. "We're working for *ourselves*. It's our only chance of getting back home."

"I think you've lost me somewhere," Jerome said, unable to accept Thwaite's words at their face value. "Home is a long way off."

"Getting the Thabbren to Earth will be only the first stage of a larger migration," Conforden said. "When the Four Thousand have been reincarnated and a Dorrinian nation established on Earth, the next step will be to build a new generation of spacecraft and begin the work of rescuing our entire population. The idea may sound hopelessly impracticable and visionary, but it can become a reality—and, naturally, Terrans who have been transferred to Dorrin will have a high priority when it comes to assigning places on the ships.

"We are the last generation of humans who will be forced to live underground on this planet." Conforden paused, then addressed himself directly to Jerome. "And you, my friend, could be back on Earth within ten years."

Chapter 7

A series of leaks had developed near Lock 18 and a maintenance crew had been sent into the section to carry out repairs.

Jerome's growing tiredness with the work was aggravated by annoyance at not being able to judge time properly. The Dorrinian "day" had nothing to do with the planet's rotation, but was a period based on circadian rhythms inherited from the legendary home world. Jerome had been told it was roughly equal to twenty-six Earth hours. As his new body had been attuned to it from birth there should have been no problems with adjustment, yet the annoyance persisted. He was accustomed to estimating work shifts in the convenient units of hours, and saw no merit in the Dorrinian system of a day which was split into a thousand undifferentiated units called mirds.

Dorrinian clocks and watches also seemed unnecessarily confusing. They operated through molecular resonances, products of the psychic micro-engineering at which the Dorrinians excelled. Their displays consisted of two rows of squarish Dorrinian digits—the upper one showing the mird count for that day, and the lower giving the number of days since the creation of the Thabbren. Other periodicities had apparently faded from the racial consciousness. Jerome found the system too linear for his liking. He missed the comforting arrangement of cycles within cycles, by which the members of his culture disguised the realities of entropy.

He also objected to working in a poorly designed vacuum suit. In the vicinity of Lock 18 the tunnel was close to the surface, and for a lengthy portion of the planetary day the temperature inside it was uncomfortably high. His suit, primitive by Terran standards, had no cooling system and even when the wearer was at rest quickly became a dank, choking autoclave. During periods of physical activity the enclosed environment was almost unbearable, but the suit was necessary in case a sudden major rupture of the tunnel wall exhausted the air.

"How are you doing, Jerome?" said Mallat Rill Glevdane, the Dorrinian who was supervising the repairs. "Problems?"

Jerome, who had been forcing mastic into a seam, paused to dab his brow through the open faceplate of his helmet. "Yes—I can't get a reliable seal here. The mastic isn't doing a lot of good."

"How much have you put in?"

"At least a kilo, and I can still hear the air going through. We ought to take the plate off and have a look at the seating."

An amused expression appeared on Glevdane's pinched face. "That's your expert opinion, is it?"

"You don't need to be an expert to see that this whole system is garbage."

"It was built forty years ago by Tarn Gall Evalne." Glevdane no longer looked amused. "He was a Guardian, and one of our most celebrated engineers."

"He might have been good at carving molecules into netsuke, but he hadn't a clue about large structures." Jerome nodded in the direction of Lock 18. "There's your trouble, right there. Rigid frames built into a semi-rigid tube. Those things are *causing* the leaks. The rest of the tunnel adapts to rock creep, but the door frames don't—so you keep on getting sprung plates."

"If the frames weren't rigid the lock doors wouldn't seal."

"Because they go *into* the frames. They should be face-fitting. I could design you an airlock door which could take a distortion of five or ten centimetres in the frame and still remain airtight."

"You must have a truly brilliant mind," Glevdane said heavily. "I wonder why it is that a man who would presume to

116

instruct Evalne has been assigned such ordinary manual work?"

"That was only because. . . ." Jerome broke off, surprised at himself—after all that had happened—for allowing old preoccupations to affect his current attitudes. Towards the end of his placement interview, sixty-six days earlier, he had been astonished to learn that his lack of formal engineering qualifications were to count against him when his place in an alien society on an alien world was being decided. It seemed monstrously unfair that the same prejudices which had worked against him on Earth could hold sway even when he was in vastly different circumstances and in another man's body on a remote planet. His youthful habit of arguing with teachers instead of listening to them was still paying a harsh return.

"Anyway," he said, "I still think the plate should come out."

"I bow to your expert opinion," Glevdane said. "Our safety regulations state that, where possible, no more than two workers shall remain in an evacuated section of the tunnel. Can you handle the job with a single helper?"

"You want *me* to do it?"

"You're the great practical engineer." Glevdane's eyes glinted in the shadowy grotto of his helmet. "Of course, if you prefer me to give the work to a more experienced. . . ."

"I can manage," Jerome said quickly, concealing his unease at the prospect of trusting his life to a Dorrinian-made vacuum suit. The limitations of the environment had had a profound effect on Dorrinian science and technology. Minerals were plentiful, but oxygen was a precious manufactured commodity and without an abundance of it there had been little progress in metallurgy. Similar constraints had affected the development of glass, plastics and other materials, with the result that many artifacts resembled museum pieces to Jerome's eyes, devices in which the greater part of the designer's ingenuity had gone into overcoming his materials' sheer unsuitability for their purpose. The garment he was wearing was a prime

117

example. To him there was more than a hint of a 19th century diving suit about it, and he suspected it would have been quite impracticable in Earth gravity.

"Very well," Glevdane said. "You have a complete tool kit here, and I'll send a man to work with you." He explained that he and the rest of the crew would observe tunnel safety regulations by withdrawing beyond two locks and sealing them before Jerome disturbed any plating.

Jerome nodded, scarcely listening, as he concentrated on checking his oxygen supply and closing up his helmet. The suit became more claustrophobic than ever when he had clamped the thick face plate, an act of imprisonment which reminded him how much he hated the Dorrinian way of life. Hardly a night ever passed without his dreaming he was back on Earth, walking in the open, feeling the benison of rain on his face, and when he awoke to the sterile warrens of the Precinct it was almost impossible to control the trembling of his limbs. The nights when Donna Sinclair was beside him were easier to bear, but the only thing which gave any direction and meaning to his existence was the long-term prospect of returning to his own world. If furthering that ambition meant working for the Dorrinians, aiding their stealthy invasion of Earth, then he was prepared to push himself to the limit.

"I volunteered to help you, Mister Jerome," said an approaching worker. "Is it okay if I help you?"

The speaker would have been practically unidentifiable in his sealed vacuum suit, but Jerome recognized the tone and mode of address. He had had a few conversations with Sammy Birkett since his arrival on Mercury, and had found them difficult and embarrassing. The young gardener appeared to have adjusted to his new circumstances with remarkable ease, but Jerome sensed an underlying confusion and terror.

One manifestation was Birkett's desire to spend as much time as possible with Jerome, talking incessantly about local affairs back in Whiteford, reciting lists of names in the hope of discovering mutual acquaintances. Jerome could sympathize,

118

but found it harrowing to remain long in Birkett's company. He and Birkett were socially incompatible, whether on Earth or on Mercury, but he had an idea that his aversion for the younger man had a lot to do with the traumatic scene in Pitman's garden. How was he to relate to a person whose face had burned outwards from the mouth, whose body had puffed and split and shrivelled in a concentration of solar fire?

"Of course you can help, Sammy," he said, resolving to make the best of the situation. "We'll show them how these things are done in Whiteford."

"You bet, Mister Jerome—we'll sure as hell show them." The suit radio, Dorrinian micro-engineering at its best, made Birkett's voice seem to originate within Jerome's helmet, creating an uncomfortable intimacy. "I'm ready to bust my ass."

"If I were you I'd avoid that kind of rhetoric," Jerome said. "Under the circumstances."

"Sorry, Mister Jerome—cussin' is just a habit with me."

"What I meant was that these suits aren't too . . . Never mind, Sammy—let's go to work."

Jerome watched Glevdane and the other members of the nine-strong work party reach Lock 17 and go through it. They closed the circular door, breaking all radio contact, and a few seconds later an amber light appeared above it, signalling that an airtight seal had been effected. There was a longer wait until the group had retreated beyond the next lock, almost two hundred metres further down the tunnel, then the image of a green circle—the Dorrinian work symbol for PROCEED —flicked briefly in Jerome's mind.

The simplified telepathic instruction from Glevdane reminded him that the two Dorrinians he had first encountered, Pitman and Belzor, were far from typical of their race in the matter of mind-to-mind communication. All Dorrinians possessed the talent to some extent, but at the median level they could do little more than transmit basic pictures to a known target at short range. With them, telepathy was simply a useful

119

adjunct to verbal communication, and they were almost as much in awe of a Pitman or a Belzor as Jerome had been when first exposed to their powers.

"Check your oxygen and we'll get started," Jerome said. He waited until Birkett had inspected his gas tank and had signalled his readiness, then began unfastening the suspect wall plate. It was held in place by slotted screws which were not significantly different from many produced on Earth. Jerome wondered if it had been a case of similar problems engendering similar solutions, or if the Terran personalities imported by telepathy over the centuries had influenced the outlook of Dorrinian designers. Aided by Birkett, he removed all the screws, inserted a lever beneath one edge of the plate and eased it up from its seating. There was an immediate screeching whistle as air began to escape to the surrounding vacuum.

Again wishing he had an Earth-style watch, Jerome counted two mirds before the sound ceased and a swelling of his suit told him the section of the tunnel had been exhausted. He imagined the unleashed molecules of air racing along the annular gap between the tunnel structure and the Mercurian rock, dispersing into crevices, and his uneasiness about the integrity of Dorrinian vacuum suits returned in force. The best that could be said for them was that they were adequate for their purpose, and he was haunted by Conforden's casual reference to the fact that eighteen workers had died in the tunnel.

With no atmospheric pressure on it the two-metre-long plate was now easier to manipulate. They peeled it away from the underlying frames and stringers, taking care not to damage the compressible seal around the edges, exposing an area of black igneous rock. It was Jerome's first direct look at the crust of the alien planet, but he was in no mood for wonderment. All his attention was focused on a slab-like fragment which had become dislodged from somewhere overhead. It had slid down the side of the tunnel and had jammed on a longitudinal, buckling the metal out of true and spoiling the air seal. The mastic Jerome had been pumping into the area was gathered on the rock in coprolitic blobs.

"Bingo," he said, feeling something of the familiar satisfaction that came from seeing through a problem and knowing it would not remain a problem for long. He gripped the rock slab and tried to lift it, but without success. The considerable mass was wedged between the longitudinal and the rock face. He moved closer, changed his hold and tried again, and had just begun to sense a movement when there came a sharp popping in his ears, signifying that his suit's internal pressure was dropping. He gave a startled grunt and leaped back from the rock as though it had stirred into hostile life. A line of brilliant red was spreading along one seam of his right gauntlet. Jerome stared at it, mesmerized, unable to breathe. After a few seconds the progress of the blood-like emergency sealant was checked and he knew that the suit had managed to heal itself. He swore bitterly and unhappily.

"What's the matter with you, Mister Jerome?" Birkett, who had been putting the separated plate aside, came within his restricted field of view. "Are you hurt?"

"The sooner we get out of these glorified union suits the better," Jerome replied. "I need help to shift this rock, but don't pull too hard or you'll pop your seams."

"It's all right, Mister Jerome—I'm a real skinny guy now, but that rock won't be no problem at all."

Birkett grappled with the dark slab, causing Jerome misgivings by putting up a great show of vigour, and helped him to lift it upwards and inwards. They set it on the tunnel floor and Jerome returned his attention to the damaged longitudinal. He was relieved to see that it had sprung back close to its original line, something he regarded as a bonus from an unsophisticated alloy. By slipping a lever between it and the rock face he was able to make further corrections, after which he began applying a run of mastic to the metal in preparation for the reseating of the plate.

121

As he worked he was continuously reminded that the tunnel was a full eight kilometres long, running from the Dorrinian capital of Cuthtranel to the expected landing site of the *Quicksilver*. To his eyes, even allowing for the difficulties under which the Dorrinians had laboured, the entire structure was crude, with engineering which would have been immediately comprehensible to a citizen of Ancient Rome. Bearing in mind the importance of the Thabbren in the Dorrinian scheme of things, he would have expected much higher standards of reliability and safety, but the project illustrated the ambivalence he had noted in the character of the Dorrinian people.

They prided themselves on being highly ethical, humane and reasonable, but at the same time they were unconsciously ruthless in any matter relating to their racial ambitions. Jerome, conditioned by his previous existence, had assumed Mercury to have a population of millions, and had been surprised to learn that the polar capital housed less than twenty thousand. There had even been periods in the millennia since the Days of the Comet when the living inhabitants of Mercury had been outnumbered by the Four Thousand whose personalities they were sworn to preserve.

Many individual sacrifices had been made in the name of the Thabbren, in pursuit of the one great objective—and the tunnel was a perfect paradigm of the racial attitudes involved. It had been constructed for the benefit of the Four Thousand, would have to serve its main function only once, and the lives of ordinary workers were expendable, provided they did not die in such numbers as to jeopardize the ultimate welfare of the Thabbren. The subterranean environment suggested an analogy to Jerome—that of soldier ants who were sacrificed for the good of the colony during the forced retreat from a nest—and in spite of the heat within his suit he could almost have shivered.

He nodded to Birkett. "Let's try the plate now, Sammy—this place is starting to have a bad effect on my nerves."

122

Birkett helped him to raise the unwieldly sheet of metal and guide it into place. Jerome was gratified to see that it fitted snugly against the underlying metal all the way around the edges. He inserted all the fixing screws and began tightening them, driving each one down until a smooth bead of mastic appeared in the adjacent seam.

"We can't leave this hunk of rock," Birkett said. "I'll take it to the buggy."

"Don't try to lift it," Jerome said, still concentrating on perfecting the edge seal. "We'll get them to bring the buggy up here."

"Goddam," Birkett grumbled. "Nobody allows me to do nothin' around here. I'm still strong as hell, you know."

"Sammy, you're not proving anything. Your present body has nothing to do with the real *you*."

"It's all right for you to talk that way, Mister Jerome. You were a brain worker and you can still do brain work. I was a gardener. What's the good of bein' a gardener in a hellhole like this?"

"Ay, there's the rub," Jerome said absently as he tightened the last screw. He took the solvent sponge out of his kit and used it to wipe the excess extruded mastic away from the edges of the refitted plate, determined to leave the job looking neat, clean and absolutely right. *Work never lets you down*, he thought, comforted by the fact that some sources of pleasure had survived transplantation.

Looking back over his time in the Precinct he was able to list a number of activities which had been satisfying and fulfilling in his previous incarnation, but which had lost their savour in his bizarre new circumstances and environment. Perhaps surprisingly, sex was among the foremost. There had been the sheer novelty of finding many women available to him—a sharp contrast to his former existence—and at first he had used physical relationships like a drug, one which helped alleviate homesickness and loneliness. Donna Sinclair, the woman he had noticed on the way to his placement interview, was his most regular partner. His second lease of youthfulness and virility was like a gift from an Arabian genie, but in keeping with fairytale morality the gift was flawed. At the height of every experience would come an intrusive series of thoughts: *Would she have done this with the real me? Would I have done it with the real her? Is that grammatical? The real she? Who are we supposed to be anyway, she and me and me and she. . . ?*

The gasp from Sammy Birkett was mingled with an explosive hiss which hurt Jerome's ears. He turned and saw Birkett, some thirty paces along the tunnel, doubling over like a man who had been shot in the midriff. The slab of rock, which he had been carrying alone, was still executing a low-gravity tumble on the floor.

"You . . . *idiot!*" Jerome ran towards Birkett, hampered by his suit, watching him sink to his knees.

"I'm sorry, Mister Jerome." Birkett's words were faint articulated sobs. "I guess . . . I guess I. . . ."

"Get in here, Glevdane," Jerome shouted. Belatedly remembering that radio contact had been lost, he tried visualizing a red triangle—the Dorrinian work symbol of an emergency—then decided it was superfluous. A man who was asphyxiating, as Birkett appeared to be doing, was bound to be telepathically conspicuous on his own. Drawing closer, Jerome saw that Birkett was clutching his left arm and was doubled over it. Judging by the quantities of crimson emergency sealant visible the material of his vacuum suit had split from the wrist to above the elbow.

Birkett looked up at Jerome and the light from a white overhead globe penetrated his face plate, revealing contorted features. His lips were moving, but so little air remained in his suit that he was producing no sound for his radio to transmit, and a second later he lost consciousness. Jerome caught the slumping body and eased it to the floor.

"Where are you, Glevdane?" he called in panic. "We need air in here!"

124

He unbuckled his equipment belt and, working clumsily because of his gloves, bound it around Birkett's upper arm with the intention of constraining the oxygen which would still be trickling from the fallen man's tank. The slick plastic material of the belt was difficult to knot tightly. He cast about him in desperation and noticed a fist-sized blob of mastic still adhering to the slab of rock. Swearing savagely all the while, he scooped up the dark grey mass, smeared it thickly around the upper end of the split in the suit's fabric and clamped down on it with both hands. He was now almost certain that Birkett's suit was airtight again and that he was in no danger as regards a supply of oxygen, but he had a grim suspicion that the principal threat lay in the complete absence of atmospheric pressure. What happened to human tissue when all external pressure was removed from it?

Jerome's alarm and feelings of helplessness grew as he realised he was dealing with a subject upon which he was quite ignorant. Were vital cells in Birkett's body invisibly rupturing? Was his blood already beginning to boil?

My God, Jerome thought strickenly, *don't tell me I'm going to have to watch the same man die twice.*

He fixed his gaze on the door of Lock 17, willing it to open or give some indication that air was being returned to his section of the tunnel. The Dorrinians had a pathological fear of vacuum and he expected them to be sluggish in reacting to a situation which involved emergency opening of any of the tunnel's multiple airlocks, but not as slow as this. Minutes were going by and there was no sign of help arriving.

Perhaps nobody is going to come! The idea was patently ridiculous, but in Jerome's state of mind it was enough to make him glance anxiously at his own oxygen meter. There was sufficient for almost forty mirds, approximately one Terran hour, so there was no real reason to fear for his own life. It was, however, hard to feel any reassurance.

On a far-off morning back in Whiteford he had taken what appeared to be a minor decision—to visit the Starzynski home

125

in person—and it had proved to be the most unfortunate action of his life. It would be quite in keeping with the pattern of events since then if he were to be unlucky enough to die as the result of an entirely avoidable accident in the tunnel which had offered his only hope of a return to Earth. The fact that the *Quicksilver* was due to touch down in only another twenty-two days, and only a few hundred metres from his present location, seemed a final and entirely appropriate touch of irony. . . .

A wrinkle appeared in the taut material covering Jerome's forearm, signifying that air was at last being bled into the tunnel section.

He had been staring at it for several seconds, cautiously withholding a sigh of relief, when it occurred to him that his improvised repair of Birkett's suit was now depriving the unconscious man of air. He released his grip and with mastic-covered fingers gently released the clamps on Birkett's face plate, at the same time becoming aware of a roaring sound from the valves of Lock 17. Birkett's suit almost immediately lost its collapsed appearance and a moment later his limbs began to twitch. His eyes opened, fixing Jerome with the bright amiable stare of a small baby.

"Sammy?" Jerome spoke uncertainly. "Are you all right?"

"I thought Doctor Bob was my friend," Birkett whispered. "He shouldn't have tricked me . . . shouldn't have done this to me . . . he just *shouldn't*. . . ."

"I think he was your friend," Jerome said, less concerned with defending Pitman than with reassuring Birkett. "I'm sure he wanted to help you."

"But I'm a *gardener*. Mister Jerome, do you really believe we're up in the sky somewhere? On Mars or some place like that?"

"I'm afraid there's no doubt that this is Mercury." Jerome, suddenly aware of the depths of Birkett's confusion, felt a pang of compassion. He had been feeling sorry for himself, but at least he had the consolation of being able to understand all that had happened to him and of knowing exactly where he was in the physical universe. It had not occurred to him that Sammy Birkett, blinkered by limited intellect, was little better off than a Dark Ages peasant for whom the translation to Mercury would have been a prolonged trip to hell.

Birkett's gaze drifted over the tunnel ceiling. "I sure hate this place."

"So do I, Sammy." Jerome forced confidence and optimism into his voice. "But some day we'll be going back to Whiteford."

"Is that the truth, Mister Jerome?"

Jerome nodded vigorously. "Why don't we make a definite arrangement to see each other every week in Cordner's and put away a pitcher or two?"

"That would be *great!*" Birkett struggled up to a sitting position and dabbed at a trickle of blood which appeared at his nose. "You and me can sit in Cordner's front bar and talk about old times."

"That's a date, but I think you'd better rest until. . . ." Jerome broke off and got to his feet as the door of Lock 17 swung open. Glevdane, distinguished by his supervisor's blue helmet came through the opening, followed by the others of the work party. He looked down at Birkett and the nearby slab of rock, then turned to Jerome.

"This is a serious incident," he said, his face hard and unfriendly. "I hope you have a good excuse."

"I've had plenty of time to think of one," Jerome snapped. "Where the hell were you?"

"We returned as quickly as possible."

"The door of Lock 16 was jammed," said a Terran member of the group, Urban Pedersen. "We had a job getting through, and the air supply in any section can only be controlled from an adjoining section. If you ask me the whole system is. . . ."

"Nobody is asking you, Pedersen," Glevdane cut in, then turned back to Jerome. "Now—what is the great practical engineer's excuse for almost letting this poor fool kill himself?"

"Who are you callin' a fool?" Birkett stood up, nearly fell and was restrained by two other workers.

"Sammy isn't a fool," Jerome said quietly. "The only mistake he made was to trust one of your vacuum suits."

"The suits were designed by Guardians."

"All that proves is. . . ." Jerome paused, sensing uncharted dangers in voicing any kind of citicism of the keepers of the Thabbren, and decided to change the subject. "Shouldn't we be getting Sammy to a doctor?"

"A medic has already been summoned," Glevdane said. "A mere Dorrinian, of course, but no doubt you will be kind enough to instruct him in his work." He turned and strode away, showing his anger by stamping the tunnel floor.

"I used to notice the same thing back on Earth," Jerome said to the other Terrans before Glevdane was out of earshot. "The more you try to help people, the less gratitude they show."

Chapter 8

The day which had begun with the near-fatal accident had been a long and tiring one, and yet at the end of it Jerome found himself unable to sleep.

It might have helped had he been able to darken his bedchamber completely, but some illumination was spilling into it from the ceiling globe in his other room—and Dorrinian light fixtures could not be extinguished. Jerome had at first been surprised by that feature, believing it to represent a considerable waste of power, then he had discovered there were no Earth-style central generating stations in Cuthtranel. The globes continuously emitted light because psi engineering had modified their molecular structure. Using the same techniques, it would have been possible to make them automatically darken themselves at "night", but the Dorrinians had phobias about darkness as well as about vacuum. The tunnel-streets of the capital—many of them as old as the pyramids—and all its dwellings were permanently washed by a chill white radiance which withered Jerome's spirit.

It would also have made sleep easier if he had been able to lie in silence, but there were no doors to serve as barriers against sound. The citizens of Cuthtranel disliked being pent up any more than the environment dictated, and their sole concessions to privacy—even for toilets and bedrooms— were blind entrances. Lying restlessly on his couch, Jerome could hear the life of the Precinct going on all around him, an unending murmur of voices punctuated by occasional laughs or distant shouts. At intervals there would be unidentifiable low-frequency sounds, rumbles and strange mechanical groans, which emanated from the heart of the city and rolled outwards through its networks of shafts and galleries.

On several occasions, soon after his translation, Jerome had walked to the central sector of Cuthtranel, motivated by curiosity and a desire to escape the confinement of the Precinct's narrow tunnels. There were no restrictions on his movements, and on his rest days he was allowed to wander at will through the huge caverns which corresponded to public squares or which housed air, water and protein production plants. Had the circumstances been different, had the old Rayner Jerome been granted a miracle holiday on Mercury, he would have found a fascinating field of study in the underground city and all the unfamiliar technologies which kept it alive. But too much had happened. His personality had been bludgeoned by monstrous events, and he was cowed and utterly depressed by the sight of thousands of human beings reduced to the scale of termites, going about their incomprehensible lives in a sunless warren. He had soon retreated to the Precinct, where he could at least have the thin comfort of hearing his own language spoken.

The dormitory section of the Precinct consisted of a main corridor, known simply as the Road, with eight numbered offshoots which were referred to as Streets. In the past the area had housed transplanted Terrans of many nationalities, but now an overwhelming proportion were from North America, Britain and Western Europe—a reflection of the fact that as their great project neared its climax the Dorrinians were concentrating their attention on the US space programme and the CryoCare organization. Jerome had been able to congratulate himself, belatedly, on having noticed the preponderance of Occidentals in the recent history of SHC during his first obsessive study of the subject. In retrospect he could see that he had been too quick to dismiss the imbalance in the statistics, but there was little ground for reproach. Although the clue had been clearly visible, nobody could possibly have guessed the fantastic truth lying behind it.

130

Looking back over the events of the day while he courted sleep, Jerome decided that it was counter-productive to keep on antagonizing the maintenance supervisor. The reason the work shift had been extended was that Glevdane had insisted on adjusting the door of Lock 16 and then on checking air valves all the way out to the far end of the tunnel. It could have been his natural reaction to the Birkett incident, but Jerome guessed the supervisor had been punishing him for continuing to be outspoken about the weaknesses of some branches of Dorrinian engineering.

The difficulties with the tunnel, Jerome had pointed out, sprang from flaws in the basic design concept. With a reliable tunnel structure there would have been no need for people in it to wear vacuum suits. Conversely, given good suits there would have been no need for the tunnel to be pressurized in the first place, and most of its maintenance problems would never have arisen.

His arguments had been countered every time by the simple statement that the system had been conceived by Guardians.

Jerome pondered tiredly on that aspect of what he was beginning to see as the typical Dorrinian mentality. He had already noted their unconscious ruthlessness as regards anything connected with the racial goal of transporting the Thabbren to Earth, and it seemed to him that Glevdane's attitude reflected the same totalitarian principles. Poor engineering was good engineering, provided the Guardians said so—a philosophy which echoed that of Earth-based regimes in which the policies of the state had been known to take precedence over scientific truth. What was it that Pirt Sull Conforden had said during his placement interview?

An overt Dorrinian presence on Earth will have tremendous potential for good.

At the time—with his mind overwhelmed by the remorseless flood of new concepts—Jerome had been inclined to accept the statement, but now . . . He tried to look into the future, to visualize a Dorrinian state newly created on Earth.

131

Where would its territories be? And did Conforden really believe that the factious nations of the third planet would welcome an alien newcomer in their midst? Was there a man, woman or child anywhere on Earth who would not feel revulsion, fear and loathing at the spectacle of four thousand revived corpses emerging from their icy stronghold to make demands on the world's fading resources?

In his weariness Jerome found the whole complex scenario too difficult to contain. On returning from work he had eaten lightly in one of the communal refectories and had gone straight to his chambers in Street Five. Art Starzynski, now a bushy-haired, doe-eyed man of about forty, had invited him to play chess, but he had refused on the grounds of his tiredness.

Starzynski had accepted his new incarnation with a great deal of stoicism, claiming that the extra decades on Mercury more than compensated for the loss of a matter of weeks on Earth, but he shared Birkett's fondness for nostalgia sessions and used chess games as occasions for reminiscing about Whiteford. Recreation of former lives was an almost universal pastime in the Precinct. In one form of the pursuit, a group who had common knowledge of a place on Earth would spend many hours drawing a wall-sized picture of it, filling in a wealth of detail, arguing pleasurably over the exact wording of a store sign or the shape of a light pole.

It was an activity which Jerome studiously avoided. He found his existence in the grey tunnels of Cuthtranel sufficiently intolerable without make-believe visits to Earth and subsequent all-too-real returns to Mercury. Similarly, he had remained aloof from all of the community activities organized under the leadership of Mel Zednik, Joe Thwaite and their committees.

The only way you'll get my support, he had once told them, *is by forming an escape committee*.

His instinctive rationale was that allowing himself to be integrated with the community life of the Precinct would mean he was accepting his lot and in some way forfeiting his right to

132

walk free on Earth. And that could never be countenanced—not even symbolically.

Conforden had spoken of the possibility of the general migration beginning after ten years. That estimate seemed wildly optimistic to Jerome, but it was a message of hope in that a term had been placed on his imprisonment, and it had given him a clear sense of purpose which was infinitely more sustaining than retrospection.

Working to the limits of his endurance had a valuable spin-off in that it usually enabled him to achieve sleep within minutes of lying down, but on this particular occasion the magic was proving ineffective. He knew from experience that it was disastrous to become irritated or to start pursuing sleep like a hunter. The trick was to relax and rid himself of all tensions, trusting nature to take its course. Sex was the classical antidote to insomnia—unhurried, peaceful and thorough love-making with a familiar partner—but Donna had told him she had other commitments for the night.

Jerome swore at himself for having let his thoughts turn in her direction, thus adding to his difficulties. She was reticent about her true age, but he suspected she had been perhaps sixty at the time of her transplantation. Her dedication to getting full value out of the lush young body she had inherited from a Dorrinian super-telepath seemed obsessive to him at times, but on this night he would have been happy to give her his full co-operation.

You're going about this the wrong way, he told himself. *If you can't stop thinking, try to regard that as a benefit. Capitalize on the excess mental energy. Try to penetrate the future. . . .*

The Thabbren was due to be placed on the surface in twenty-two days' time, and soon after that the *Quicksilver* would reach Mercury and manoeuvre into a polar orbit. It gave Jerome a curious poignant thrill to visualize the tiny shell of metal which at that very moment was slowly overtaking Mercury as it hurtled around the Sun.

The three men on board had taken many weeks to accom-

133

plish the journey he had completed between heartbeats, and for one of them it was actually a return trip. Astronaut Charles Baumanis, as he was known on Earth, was a Dorrinian super-telepath who had made the mental transfer twelve years ago. After touchdown, and while his two companions were concentrating their attention on the supposed fragment of an interstellar ship, he would stray a short distance to where the Thabbren was waiting and surreptitiously put it in his pocket. Few people apart from Guardians had ever seen the repository of the Four Thousand, but Jerome had been told that it resembled a small opal. It was a paradox of the Dorrinian mind that their psychic engineering talents enabled them to perform the incredible feat of storing four thousand human personalities within the molecules of a single crystal, while at the same time they turned out large-scale artifacts which could have been bettered by Henry Ford.

The lenticular jewel of the Thabbren had been set in a ring of platinum so that the Dorrinian, Rithan Tell Marmorc, would be able to transport it inconspicuously to the CryoCare base. Jerome could picture the projected train of events up to that point, but his imagination baulked at trying to encompass what would follow. . . .

"May I come in?" The woman who spoke was standing in the doorless arch of the entrance to his room.

"Why so formal all of a sudden?" Jerome raised himself on one elbow, startled but relieved that Donna had changed her plans, then saw that the silhouette in the doorway was of a young woman in Dorrinian dress. "I . . . Do I know you?"

"We met before—once. My name is Avlan Fell Commelva." The woman advanced to the side of his couch and stood looking down at him. Her face would probably have been pretty in the harsh light of the corridors, and in the subdued illumination of the bedchamber it had the inhuman beauty of an Ancient Egyptian princess. The expression was enigmatic, a blend of hunger and disdain.

"I'm afraid I don't remember," Jerome said, drawing him-

134

self up to a sitting position from which he could get a better look at his visitor. The ribbon blouses worn by Dorrinians of both sexes were without practical function, no covering being necessary in the hothouse conditions of Cuthtranel, and in this case the blue-grey strips had parted to reveal the woman's breasts. Jerome felt organic switches click all through his body as he saw that her nipples were erect.

"I was in the recovery room when you transferred," the woman said.

Jerome called up a memory image of his first moments on Mercury, again saw a woman covering her face, being led away in obvious distress. "I think I understand."

"I've been avoiding you ever since." The woman's voice was low and intense. "I loved Orkra Blamene—and I hated you for invading his body."

"I didn't have much choice in the matter."

"That goes without saying. I was out of my mind." Avlan slowly extended one hand and touched Jerome's face, tentatively, as though half-expecting her fingers to encounter nothingness. "I couldn't bear to think about Orkra at first, then I began to feel that *I* would be taking part in his murder if I denied he had ever existed. I'm learning to enjoy my memories of him, and I want to enjoy them to the full—but it isn't fair to you."

"The honesty makes it fair," Jerome said, lying back on the couch. "Well . . . more fair than anything else that has happened to me recently."

"Thank you." Avlan paused in the act of unfastening her skirt. "I might call you Orkra."

Jerome thought about the wife who had been part of another and far-off existence. "That's all right—I might get your name wrong as well."

Chapter 9

"I've been getting quite a few reports about you, Rayner." Pirt Sull Conforden's face was thoughtful, the pale flawless skin glowing like eggshell in the light of the overhead globe. "I hear you don't get on very well with your supervisors."

Jerome sighed. "If it's Glevdane you're talking about—I apologize. I wasn't trying to needle him. He's a bit too chauvinistic."

"It isn't possible for a Dorrinian to be chauvinistic. By criticizing the work of the Guardians you appear to criticize the Guardians themselves—and, by inference, the Four Thousand."

Where's my dictionary of diplomatic answers? Jerome thought. "I'm sorry. My sole concern was with getting the Thabbren safely to Earth." He glanced across at Zednik and Thwaite, who had assembled in the small room to replicate his original placement interview. Their faces were solemn and carefully neutral, but he could sense the animosity in Zednik.

"I'll accept that as the truth, without going too far into your motivation," Conforden said.

"There's no secret about my motivation—it's the same as yours," Jerome replied. "I want to get away from this rattery some day."

"You should show some respect for the Director." Zednik scowled at Jerome as he spoke, the lines of his forehead deepening into razor slashes.

Jerome nodded to him in mock-politeness. There had been antagonism between them since their first meeting, largely because of Jerome's refusal to recognize the older man's mayoral authority. Zednik had been deputy sheriff of a small town in Florida at the time of his translation in the 1950s, and had spent four decades industriously playing civics in the Precinct. Jerome, refusing to treat the place as anything but a prison, had not joined the game.

"It's all right, Mel—I'm becoming accustomed to Rayner's mode of speech." Conforden turned his eyes to Jerome. "It has also been reported to me that you work extra shifts in the tunnel."

Jerome nodded. "Same motivation."

"And that quick action on your part saved a man's life."

"I don't want any medals puncturing my vacuum suit," Jerome said. "What's this all about?"

"The Thrabbren is being placed on the surface tomorrow. Only Guardians are permitted to go near it, of course, but I have decided to give you a place in the accompanying work party." Conforden produced a wry smile. "The rest of us see this as a great honour, but you may look on it as a major step on the road back to Earth. Do you want the appointment?"

"Always willing to oblige," Jerome said, concealing the lust that had suddenly been born inside him, the craving to raise his head and see *beyond* a horizon and into the beckoning depths of space. It might even be possible to pick out a glimmer of light from Earth itself—oceans, mountains, pastures, cities with parks and libraries and all-night grocery stores—all compressed into a single spark and fine-drawn into a bright thread of photons linking him with home. At that moment he could think of no greater reward for his labours.

"Pardon me, Director, but this isn't according to the decisions we minuted at the last Precinct Council meeting," Zednik said. "My understanding was that I would select the Terran representative for the Thabbren escort. In my opinion the honour should go to the worker with the longest service in the tunnel."

Conforden nodded, but in disagreement. "We're not talking about a ceremonial parade. Rayner may be useful in some small way, and that is the overriding consideration—although

137

it is quite inconceivable that anything could go wrong with the Guardians' plans at this stage."

You should never say things like that, Jerome thought, watching the interplay of excitement and pride on Conforden's young-old face. *It was hubris that got me where I am today.*

Chapter 10

For more than a day there had been nothing to do but wait, watch and think—and it was a time of utter strangeness.

After having adjusted to being on another world and to inhabiting a different body, Jerome had supposed himself immune to feelings of wonder—but this was a distillation of strangeness, a coming together and a culmination of every outré aspect of his new existence.

From where he sat on a portable chair he could see, to his left, the enigmatic, vacuum-suited figures of the six Guardians whose duty it had been to transport the Thabbren the full length of the tunnel and place it on the airless surface of the planet. Pirt Conforden was sitting among them, but in the half-light of the large terminal chamber it was impossible to pick him out from the others.

To Jerome's right were the eight tunnel engineers, including Mallat Glevdane, who had been responsible for the tedious opening and closing of airlocks during the eight-kilometre journey from Cuthtranel. They were sitting near the cluster of small electric vehicles which had carried the party, and which also housed food supplies and toilet facilities.

There was a minimum of movement, and conversation was limited to brief whispered exchanges. All eyes were fixed on a large screen which was permanently attached to one wall of the chamber. The image it bore was of the Mercurian surface, so perfectly portrayed that at times Jerome felt he was looking through a picture window. It was a deep-focus view of a rocky plain, bound by jagged escarpments and illuminated by fierce horizontal rays from a sliver of unbearable brilliance on the horizon. Stars shone in a black sky, seemingly more numerous when farther from the Sun.

Jerome knew that the moon-like scene actually existed over his head, ten metres above the chamber, but he had yet to find out how it was being reproduced. Television and conventional photographic techniques were not involved, that much he knew, and he guessed that Dorrinian psychic engineers had simply arranged for the molecules of the screen to react in sympathy with others on the surface. The "camera" may have been a normal-seeming patch of rockface linked to the screen by a kind of inorganic telepathy. Totally impossible to detect, it was a perfect example of what the super-telepathic elite could do best.

Clearly visible in the middle distance were the gleaming metallic curvatures of the decoy—the huge sheet of alloy which had successfully lured a ship into crossing millions of kilometres of interplanetary space. It had been brought out of the tunnel in sections four years earlier and assembled by workers who had then used gas jets to obliterate all their footprints.

And in the centre of the foreground was the Thabbren—the most complex single artifact ever produced by human beings, the living jewel which had shaped the history of two worlds for more than three millennia.

Jerome, hoping for a direct glimpse of the Thabbren, had been disappointed to find it was encased in a protective covering which closely resembled a white pebble about the size of a golfball. Even if Marmorc were to be seen picking it up he would be able to pass it off as a mildly interesting rock specimen and await his chance to extract the fantastic kernel in seclusion. It was visible on the screen as a white fleck, carefully placed midway between two distinctive boulders which resembled human skulls. Marmorc probably had studied the small patch of ground before his translation to Earth, carrying every detail of it in his memory during his years of astronaut training, although as a super-telepath he could have been directed to the Thabbren by the Guardians watching from below.

Not having thought too much about the matter, Jerome had been surprised when, after the uneventful placing of the Thabbren by two Guardians, the entire group had remained in the terminal chamber to watch it—even though the *Quicksilver* had not been due to land for two days. From the little he knew about the Guardians it had seemed quite natural for them to segregate themselves in one part of the chamber, but he had been a little taken aback when the ordinary engineers, with whom he had worked closely, had isolated him from their company. Only when the vigil had been under way for some hours, giving him time to think and absorb its emotional qualities, had it dawned on him that the occasion was essentially religious in nature.

The bleakly alien environment, the dehumanizing vacuum suits, the low-pulsing engines and the rubbery smell of manufactured oxygen—all these had blinded him to the realization that for the Dorrinians, here was Bethlehem. And Mecca. And Teotihuacán. And Buddh Gaya. As he sat apart in the cavernous twilight, watching the watchers, it came to Jerome that no Earthly religion could have offered its devotees an experience of like intensity. Thirty-five centuries of effort and suffering had narrowed down and focused on this climactic event, an inconceivably massive inverted pyramid of time grinding down on a single point—and there was no guarantee that the load could be sustained. The classical Terran religions offered certitude, the commodity common to all, but there was a fearsome element of chance shot through this holiest moment in Dorrinian history.

Jerome was observing the ultimate gamble. The collective Dorrinian soul, encapsulated in a gem, was exposed on the meteor-scarred plain waiting to be transported to Heaven-on-Earth. But there would be no divine courier to ensure its safety. Instead, a complex and comparatively primitive spacecraft would grope its way down out of the void under

141

the fallible control of men and their machines. The failure of any one of ten thousand components manufactured anywhere from Seattle to Milan to Nagasaki could terminate the ship's mission at any time, thus slamming the doors of futurity on an entire race. Where a Christian placed his trust in the Cross, a Dorrinian was required to have faith that no microscopic circuit was developing a submicroscopic lesion, that no rivets in the *Quicksilver*'s flimsy structure had been given improper heat treatment.

What will they do if something goes wrong? Jerome thought. He considered the question for a short time and in his growing tiredness found it just as intractable as the other problem whose perplexities still lingered in his mind. It was impossible for him to visualize the pattern of events which would be consequent on everything going right for the Dorrinians. He closed his eyes, shutting out the distractions of the unearthly scene, and allowed himself to drift, wondering at his ability even to contemplate sleep when the fate of two worlds was about to be decided. . . .

There were no sounds of alarm—but the feeling was unmistakable.

Jerome snapped his eyes open, responding to the psychic turbulence, and scanned his surroundings. Instinct caused him to direct his attention to the panoramic image on the screen, but it was as lifeless and changeless as ever; then he noticed that one of the Guardians had crossed the chamber and was talking quietly to the group of tunnel technicians. Jerome guessed that the speaker was Conforden, whose duty it was to act as an interface between the Guardians and other Dorrinians. Ostensibly there was nothing disturbing in that, but his yammering sense of unease persisted. Toying with the idea that his inherited neural complex might have retained some telepathic ability, he watched Conforden closely until the muted conversation had ended. He waited until Conforden was returning to his place with the Guardians, then stood up quickly and intercepted him.

"It's bad manners to whisper in company, Pirt," he said. "You told me there were no secrets on Dorrin."

"I thought you were sleeping," Conforden replied. The raised circular faceplate of his helmet was haloed with reflections, and his face was almost invisible in the shaded aperture below.

"I was resting my eyes. Is there a problem?"

Conforden appeared to weigh the question. "We have just picked up some news broadcasts from Earth. The *Quicksilver* has reported that Baumanis is ill."

"Is this on the radio? I didn't know you listened on the radio."

"It's the easiest method of getting information," Conforden said, moving on his way. "Take our word for it."

Jerome side-stepped to maintain the contact. "Are you worried about him, Pirt? Do you think it's serious, your man being sick?"

"I thought you understood these things by this time." Conforden's voice was oddly wooden. "A Dorrinian with Marmorc's powers never has an illness."

"So what's the explanation?"

"You have already met the explanation," Conforden said, placing one hand flat on Jerome's chest as a signal that he was prepared to say no more. "The Prince has grown stronger than we knew."

Jerome stared at Conforden's retreating figure, too numbed to go after him or call out. Now and then during his time in Cuthtranel he had thought about Prince Belzor—always with a frisson of dread as he recalled the baleful eyes and the pallid, implacable face—but somehow he had relegated him to the past. Perhaps his subconscious had decreed that he had too much to contend with as it was, predisposing him to a woolly optimism which assured him the Prince would have no further influence over his fate.

But now, without warning, the situation had changed.

143

A bleak new version of reality was obtruding, one in which Jerome's hopes for the future were revealed as foolishly ill-founded, impossibly precarious. Believing that his eventual return to Earth was threatened by nothing more than the possible unreliability of a spacecraft had been naïvety. It appeared that the ominous Prince Belzor, the Dorrinian superman who had come so close to obliterating Jerome, was now intent on condemning him to . . . to . . . The thought was insupportable. Jerome's mind rebelled against even visualizing a lifetime in the hopeless sterility of the Precinct. The life that would be one endless, silent scream.

"Don't just walk away like that, Pirt," he pleaded, breaking the petrifying spell. "What are you talking about? What can Belzor *do* at this range?"

Conforden continued walking and joined the knot of five other Guardians. They had risen to their feet and were standing close together, possibly in telepathic communion, the bulkiness of their vacuum suits disguising the proportion of men to women. These were the enigmatic mandarins of Dorrinian society, remote and venerated entities, regarded as direct instruments of the Four Thousand. An ordinary Dorrinian might speak to one only once in his life, and even then with many elaborate preliminaries, but Jerome was a driven man. He strode towards the Guardians, waving his arms to gain their attention. Conforden looked around, saw him coming and quit the group to bar his way.

"Stay back," he whispered urgently. "You don't know what you're doing."

"That's the trouble." Finding himself unable to pass the Dorrinian, Jerome raised his voice. "I don't know what *anybody's* doing around here. What's all this crap about Belzor? I demand to. . . ." He broke off, confounded, as one of the Guardians turned to face him and even in the darkness of the helmet's maw he saw the eyes begin to lase and felt the blossoming of pain, the special pain. . . .

More than two thousand years of life have not been enough to satisfy the Prince. Indeed, his appetites are greater than ever. And now that he feels threatened he has become a monster in human form. He is clever, egotistical, amoral, ruthless, and dangerous. Above all, he is dangerous—the ultimate threat to the future of the Dorrinian race.

As soon as the Prince identified Rithan Tell Marmorc, incarnated on Earth as Charles Baumanis, as the Guardian who would transport the Thabbren to Earth he set out to destroy him. He was the cause of two fatal accidents on Quicksilver training missions, but Marmorc managed to escape each time. The Prince then devised a new form of attack. His enormous life-span has enabled him to develop his psychic powers to an unprecedented extent, and he began using them to mount a direct telepathic assault on Marmorc. His method was to drive a needle cone of mind-energy through Marmorc's personal defences, to disrupt and dissipate Marmorc's kald.

The plan almost succeeded. Marmorc came near to death, but he was saved because such an attack is as directional as a laser beam, and other Guardians were able to interpose themselves between the Prince and Marmorc. Four of them died before the Guardians could assemble in sufficient numbers to nullify Belzor's power. From that time onwards, until he boarded the Quicksilver, Marmorc was protected continuously by a ring of Dorrinian super-telepaths. There was a brief period when it was even hoped that Belzor himself might be destroyed, because he could not attack again without betraying his own position, and by then many Guardians were mobilized and ready to go against him. He was, however, too wary to make that mistake.

Instead, he resorted for a time to the tactic he has employed against Guardians in the past—random, widely-separated attacks, often involving the use of conventional weapons, against Dorrinians, especially those who were important to the Cryo-Care organization. He then ceased his activities and dropped out of sight, and it was assumed that he was gathering his resources for a final onslaught, centred either on Marmorc *when he returned to Earth or on the CryoCare base in the Antarctic.*

It was also assumed that while Marmorc was on his inter-planetary voyage he could not be harmed by the Prince, because of the supposed impossibility of focusing a kald lens on a small, remote, invisible and rapidly moving object.

That was the biggest and most disastrous error the Guardians have ever made in their dealings with the Prince.

We now realize that he has been refining his powers, developing capabilities which even the most advanced Dorrinian tele-paths can scarcely comprehend. At this very instant—in spite of the astronomical distance which separates them—he is dissipating Marmorc's kald, siphoning away his life energies, and unless he can be stopped Marmorc will die and the Thabbren may never reach Earth.

The attack on Marmorc is as directional as the previous one, but in this case the needle cone is being directed upwards from the surface of the Earth—which means that it cannot be intercepted or used to pinpoint Belzor's position. We believe that he must be in a location from which he can maintain uninterrupted line-of-sight contact with Mercury/Dorrin for many hours, which indicates—as it is now summer in the Earth's southern hemisphere—somewhere in Antarctica. Many Dorrinians have gone there in search of him, prepared for a fight to the death, but it is a large continent, and the time left to us is very short.

The future of our entire race hangs by the slenderest thread. . . .

. . . SO BE SILENT AND BE STILL!

Jerome was only dimly aware of having folded at the knees, of having been helped back to his chair by Conforden. He had learned earlier that telepathy was partly a physical process, involving the teleportation of electrical charges into the receiver's brain, which accounted for the stunning effect of the fleeting mental contact with the Guardian. But there had also been a devastating emotional component superimposed on the informational content of the transfer. For a single instant he had felt what the Dorrinians were feeling, had shared their agonies as the millennia-long racial dream was suddenly threatened with dissolution, had seen himself as a blundering and sacrilegious intruder.

He sat back in the chair, breathing deeply and trying to regain his equilibrium. There had been callousness in the way the Guardian had treated him, but he consoled himself with the reflection that on Earth lesser men would have killed him for the same kind of interference in an infinitely lesser crisis. The Guardians were still standing in a tight group, motionless as statues, and he could only speculate about the telepathic conflict in which they were engaged.

Were they, by means he would never understand, endeavouring to shield the Dorrinian on board the spacecraft? Were they in communication with their agents in the distant snowfields of Antarctica? Or were they striving to forge their kald lenses into a single insubstantial spear which could stab down through the Earth's atmosphere and transfix the renegade Prince? Was there a possibility that Belzor could strike back at them with his incredible powers, destabilizing their needle cones of mental energy into oscillating spheres which encompassed the Sun? Might the psi gladiators suddenly burst into flame?

Awed by the sheer scope of the silent conflict, chastened by his inability to penetrate its mysteries, Jerome lapsed into a kind of gloomy watchfulness. The group of Dorrinian technicians to his right appeared to be similarly subdued. There was little activity among them and even the whispered conversations had died out. All eyes were fixed on the screen's unchanging image of the Mercurian surface, on the white speck of the Thabbren, and the atmosphere in the chamber was one of intense, brooding apprehension. In the absence of movement, the viscosity of time seemed to increase, insensibly thickening around the watchers, smothering them in its cold clear amber.

147

This is never going to end, Jerome thought. *We'll be here for ever. . . .*

The *Quicksilver* came down so rapidly that Jerome almost believed it was out of control.

He leaped to his feet, mouth agape in readiness to shout a futile warning, then he saw the dust clouds which told him the ship's landing jets were in operation. The flat billows, lacking air to buoy up their separate particles, dropped in an instant like heavy blankets—and, magically, the spacecraft from Earth had arrived.

It sat on the Mercurian plain, an angular edifice on a landing tripod, harshly illuminated from one side, reminding Jerome of an etched illustration in a 19th century scientific romance. The launching from Earth orbit, coupled with the use of high-efficiency, state-of-the-art engines, had enabled the mission planners to forget the astronaut's nightmare of orbital rendezvous at destination. It had not been necessary to have a mother ship dispatch a landing module to the planetary surface. Instead, the *Quicksilver* itself—big as a truck, bristling with antennae, exuding the confidence of reserve power—had taken up a solid stance on the surface of an alien planet. It had touched down about a hundred metres away from the Dorrinian sensor, squarely in the flat and boulder-free area which had led to the selection of the decoy site.

Looking at the ship, Jerome was overwhelmed by a surge of pride and homesickness which simultaneously closed his throat and blurred his vision. He took a single step, a lover's faltering step, towards the image on the screen, then it came to him that nobody else in the chamber had moved or acknowledged the momentous event in any way. The Guardians were a statuary group of six on his left; the other Dorrinians were dispersed among the vehicles, dimly-seen mannikins, seemingly devoid of life.

Marmorc must be all right, Jerome told himself. *If the worst had happened, if he had died, the Guardians would have known about it, and I would have seen some reaction from somebody.*

Either way—they should be responding to my beautiful ship.

Damn them, they should be wringing their hands, or ringing their bells.

Jerome turned his eyes back to the screen, baffled and embarrassed, and felt a tingle of surprise as he saw that, although not more than a minute had elapsed since touchdown, a hatch in the *Quicksilver*'s side was swinging open. He had expected the astronauts to spend many hours on checks and tests before they took the major step of unsealing the ship. Was this an emergency procedure? Under Jerome's mesmerized gaze, a telescopic ladder was extended from the dark square of the hatch. As soon as it had reached the ground a figure in a white spacesuit appeared at the top. One of the Guardians near Jerome gave a low gasp.

That's Marmorc, Jerome thought as the astronaut slid down the ladder, keeping his feet clear of the rungs. His knees buckled as he impacted with the ground. He pulled himself upright with obvious difficulty, leaned his head against the ladder for a moment, then turned and stumbled towards the Thabbren, a direction which meant he was facing the underground watchers. After only a few paces he began to weave from side to side. Beyond him, two other men emerged from the spacecraft and swarmed down the ladder.

The first man's course became more and more erratic and his progress slower until, at last, he came to a halt and stood swaying. His face was masked by moonscape reflections, but it was apparent that he was being overtaken by a personal catastrophe. He spread his arms, stood perfectly still for a second, then collapsed with the utter, slack-jointed finality of a puppet whose strings have been sheared.

Somewhere in the terminal chamber a Dorrinian emitted a wail of anguish—a thin, keening sound unlike anything Jerome had ever heard before, expressive of a pain and heartsickness beyond human endurance. The harrowing sound was

149

echoed by others, swelling in volume until the chamber rang with it, sang with it, exerting a terrible pressure within Jerome's head. Over to his left, a Guardian toppled sideways and was caught and lowered to the floor by his companions.

"No," Jerome breathed. "No, no, *no!*"

He backed away from the screen, which now showed the remaining two astronauts bending over the inert figure of Marmorc, and kept moving without looking around—guided by a radar-like awareness of his surroundings—until his hands encountered metal projections. Moving as in a dream, he turned and drove the engineer's key attached to his belt into the lock of the tunnel door. It rotated easily. He threw the dogging lever, hauled the door open a short way and squeezed through the gap into the tunnel which ran from the terminal chamber to the surface.

The single globe in the tunnel roof splayed light into the dimness of the chamber, causing the nearest Dorrinians to turn in his direction.

Jerome slammed the door with all his strength and dogged it shut. This part of the tunnel was only about forty metres in length and ascended steeply to the surface. Jerome had not been in it before, but he knew that it contained two further airtight doors, for safety, and that the section beyond the nearer of them had been evacuated. He ran up the slope to the door, clamping the faceplate of his helmet down as he went, and had to stab three times with his key before managing to guide it into the lock of the equalizer valve. Air whistled through the valve as he twisted it to the open position.

He unlocked the dogging lever, threw it and—unable to restrain himself—tried to drag the door open at once. Still clamped in place by air pressure differential, it resisted his efforts. Jerome let go of the handle, suddenly fearful of rupturing his glove, and forced himself to remain motionless while the equalizer valve did its work. The ten or twelve seconds that it took passed with nightmarish slowness, and in the nightmare he was overtaken and brought down many

150

times by pursuing Dorrinians. When the sound of escaping air became inaudible he pulled the door open and ran up the incline to the one which formed the end of the tunnel proper.

This time the rush of air was less violent when he opened the valve, the pressure in the tunnel having been halved. He began to feel safer, knowing that the door to the terminal chamber now could not be opened until every Dorrinian beyond it had sealed his vacuum suit. He opened the final door, crouched down and stepped through into a small cell which had been hewn into dark basalt. In its roof was ribbed panel of dull plastic which closely resembled, the surrounding rock. He put his hands on the panel and pushed upwards. It lifted easily and slid away to one side, and he found himself looking into a black and star-seeded sky.

He climbed up out of the cell and stood up on a gently sloping crown of rock, the cuboidal cracking of which had effectively disguised the tunnel entrance hatch. The scene before him was exactly what he had observed from the underground chamber, all its elements assembled on a natural stage.

Most distant was the complex boxy shape of the *Quicksilver*, and close to it was the mirrored metal of the decoy which the Dorrinians had assembled on the surface at such a great cost in human lives. In the centre of the arena the two astronauts were kneeling by their fallen companion, and closest to Jerome—flanked by two skull-shaped boulders—was an insignificant-looking white pebble containing the soul of a beleaguered race.

The whole, with its background of scarps and crater walls, was starkly lit by the paring of the Sun's disc which blazed on the horizon, and low in the sky was a twinned speck of blue-white brilliance. In spite of its remoteness, the Earth-Moon system was an integral part of the tableau. Not only was it the ultimate goal for Jerome and every Dorrinian, it was the emplacement from which Belzor, the malign superman, had struck down a chief actor in the drama which was being enacted. Jerome visualized him somewhere in the white

151

wilderness of the Antarctic, perhaps lying on his back in a thermal cocoon, his unblinking gaze fixed on Mercury as he drove a lance of psychic power through millions of kilometres of space. . . .

Tranced and bemused, Jerome replaced the hatch behind him and stepped down off the dome of rock. He felt no sensation in his body or limbs—he had become a pair of eyes, a discorporate being floating through a dream landscape. The white pebble containing the Thabbren was just ahead, calling to him. He picked it up and dropped it into the thigh pocket of his right leg and continued walking towards the Terran astronauts.

Their attention was concentrated on Marmorc as they began to lift the body, and Jerome was only a few paces away when one of them turned his head and saw him. The astronaut released Marmorc and sprawled backwards, cowering away from Jerome. His mouth was wide open, and in the airless silence Jerome was slow to realize the man was screaming. The other astronaut was on his feet and backing away, his hands outstretched as though to ward off a blow.

Jerome, recovering the ability to empathize with his own kind, suddenly understood that he had given the two men the worst shock they were ever likely to experience. They had just completed a three-month voyage to an alien world and had been in a state of high anxiety over their crewmate—and if there was anything which was *not* supposed to happen it was the sudden appearance of a humanoid figure in a strange design of spacesuit. Jerome took a step backwards and raised his hands, hoping to convey reassurance, then he realized he was beginning to hear the laboured breathing of the two men. The button-sized Dorrinian transceiver in his helmet was tuning itself to the frequency used by the astronauts' suit radios.

"I'm from Earth," he said quickly, grateful that micro-communication was one of the fields in which the Dorrinians excelled. "Everything is all right. I'm like you. I'm from Earth."

"The hell you are," one of the astronauts gasped. "Stay away from me."

152

"I know you've had a shock—and I apologize—but please take some time to think." Jerome paused, becoming aware of a problem he would have to solve within the next minute. "Look, I speak English, and I even know your names. You are Hal Buxton and Carl Teinert—although I don't know which is which. Take a minute and think about it."

There was a period of silence during which the recumbent astronaut slowly got to his feet. The two men faced Jerome warily, and he prayed they would not be able to think too logically about his words. By identifying them as Buxton and Teinert he had revealed foreknowledge that the dead astronaut was Marmorc/Baumanis.

"Okay, we've thought about it," the taller of the two men said. "Now tell us who the hell you are and how you got here."

Everything that had happened to Jerome since that prehistoric morning when, in all his innocence and ignorance, he had driven to Pitman's house sped through his mind . . . strange images and outlandish concepts blurring in a praxinoscope of memory. The universe was waiting for him to speak.

"My name is Pavel Radanovik," he said steadily. "I hold the rank of captain in the air force of the Union of Soviet Socialist Republics."

The Americans glanced at each other, then scanned the horizon. "Where's your ship?"

"What remains of it is lying in a ravine about twenty kilometres from here. It developed a guidance fault at a late stage of the descent. My three comrades died in the crash."

"I never heard anything so. . . ." The American who was doing the talking swung his arms out and let them fall to his side, conveying his exasperation. "And how did you get here?"

"I walked, of course," Jerome said. "I was able to carry spare oxygen cylinders—enough to get me here—then I waited for you to arrive."

"Where are the cylinders?"

"I was discarding them as they went down. I'm wearing the last one now. You got here just in time."

153

"Hell, this is the Goddamnest. . . ."

"We're forgetting about Charlie," the shorter astronaut cut in, speaking for the first time. "I think he's dead, Hal. He told us he was going to die—and he did it. This is really weird."

"You're telling me," Hal Buxton replied, his gaze still locked on Jerome's face. There was a perplexity in his eyes, a deep uneasiness, and Jerome knew exactly what was causing it. Two highly unusual events had happened almost simultaneously, and although it was patently impossible to connect them there was a voice whispering inside the astronaut's head, a persuasive voice telling him there *had* to be a connection. That voice was well known to Jerome. It was the one which had assured him there had to be a link between cases of spontaneous human combustion, and he did not want Buxton to continue listening to it.

"Don't look at me that way," he said, projecting all the sincerity he could muster. "What possible reason could I have for lying to you?"

Chapter 11

The Earth, as seen from the *Quicksilver*'s observation ports, was more vast than Jerome could have anticipated.

It curved away from him on all sides in rolling blue-white vistas which occupied almost half the sky, its hugeness emphasized by the incredible amount of detail on show. Individual clouds could be seen like grains of powder which had been stirred into spirals on a blue ceramic platter, and where land masses were visible the mind supplied a million fractals for even the smallest feature. The outline of the North American continent, with all its school atlas associations, held Jerome's attention for hours at a time as he went on imaginary drives from one well-remembered region to another.

His homesickness had increased steadily during the three months of the return journey, and now that the *Quicksilver* was actually in Earth orbit he had an addict's craving to regain the life he had known. Intellectually he knew it was impossible— the change in his appearance alone was enough to guarantee that—but the heart is more stubborn than the mind. In dreams and daydreams he browsed in Whiteford's bookshops, strolled the familiar streets, replanted his lawn with the best imported dwarf grass, took time for art classes in the ivy-clad Methodist College. . . .

And when wide awake he found it hard to believe he was in the final hours of the flight from Mercury to Earth.

Looking back over the three months he had spent locked in a small cabin with two other men he was able to identify the factors which had made the journey bearable. Foremost among them was the friendship he had developed with

Buxton and Teinert, although the relationship—naturally enough— could hardly have had a less promising start.

Some of the initial friction might have been avoided had he been able to help in the burial of the man they knew as Charles Baumanis. It had taken more than two hours for the astronauts to get their radioed reports accepted by anybody in the Spacex Corporation's operational HQ in Florida, and they had been caught in a personal dilemma by the first clear instruction regarding Baumanis: *Discard the body and proceed with your mission.*

The mission controllers, secure in their bounteous home environment, had failed to understand the psychology of remoteness, of men whose ties with the rest of humanity had been stretched invisibly thin. A dead comrade *had* to be buried, and with all due honour. There was no other way.

Jerome understood that better than Buxton and Teinert knew, but by then he had been running out of oxygen and compelled to take refuge in the ship. At that point the astronauts had been faced with another problem which was connected with the ungovernable fears of the space traveller. They had solved it by placing Jerome in the dead man's seat and securely tying his hands and feet. Even with that safeguard they kept glancing at the ship all the while they were gathering stones and raising a cairn over Baumanis's body, and Jerome knew what was going through their minds. It was virtually impossible for him to get free of his bonds, even more impossible for him to fly the *Quicksilver* alone, but he was *in* the ship and they were *out* of it, and Earth was very far away, and space always kills when it can.

The pure symbolism of his assisting in the burial would have been significant. Large and versatile though the *Quicksilver* was compared to the Moon landers of thirty years earlier, it could not have taken four men back to Earth. As Buxton and Teinert saw it, for logic has no place in such matters, their friend's life had been traded for that of a stranger, and some innermost part of them would have been mollified if he could have been seen to pay his last respects by the grave. In the rich social matrix of the home world the consideration would have scarcely arisen, but at the far point of a billion-kilometre round trip it was important.

Other difficulties had arisen from his snap decision to claim to be a Soviet cosmonaut. It had not been so much a question of ideology and national stances—the remoteness of Earth had been a bonus in that respect—but the restraint on his natural honesty. Having told the basic lie, he had been forced to use it as the cornerstone of a complex structure of lies about his boyhood on the shores of the Sea of Okhotsk, his family and friends, and his military career. An excellent memory for detail had enabled him to maintain the deception. Buxton was from Tulsa and Teinert from a small town in Idaho, and they liked to tell rambling yarns about their early lives to pass the long watches of the mid-voyage. The communions had formed a vital part of the three-cornered friendship, and Jerome's sense of guilt had increased every time he invented a good embellishment or a specially convincing detail for his own fictional past.

Gazing down on the convex panoramas of Earth, he wondered if he would ever have the chance to speak truthfully to the two spacemen and dispel some of the mysteries which otherwise were going to haunt them till they died. They had, for example, spent many hours trying to work out an explanation for what had happened with Baumanis. There had been no physical symptoms of illness, but in the late stages of the flight Baumanis had grown more and more listless and withdrawn. Just before touchdown at Mercury's north pole he had appeared to be delirious, though with no fever, and had uttered some fragmented sentences, apparently vowing to hang on to life for the extra minutes it would take to reach "home". They had been shocked to realize the extent of his mental deterioration and had decided to put him under sedation, but Baumanis had pleaded with such sudden intensity that they had chosen to let him do exactly as he wished during what were to be his last few minutes.

157

Jerome—keeper of many secrets—had consoled himself
with the reflection that, even if he had been free to speak, the
truth about Baumanis would have received as little credence
as the truth about the opal ring he wore on his left hand.

He had quite expected the Thabbren's pebble-like container to be difficult and perhaps impossible for him to open,
but it had split readily along an invisible seam on the first
application of tension. It had then occurred to him that the
container might be a good example of Dorrinian mind-to-
matter engineering. Had he not been accepted as an instrument of the Guardians the pebble might have remained as
obdurate as the real thing, protecting its contents from pro-
fane eyes for a further thousand years if necessary. And in
spite of his desire that things should be otherwise, there had
been a strong element of the quasi-religious in the awe
Jerome had experienced on actually seeing and touching the
Thabbren itself.

Floating in the dimness of the *Quicksilver*'s cabin, while
the two astronauts drowsed in their restraint nets, Jerome
had been numbed and humbled by the sight of the lenticular
opal into which had been concentrated the past and future of
an entire race. The varicoloured motes within it seemed to
shine with a light of their own, and to move and change even
when the ring itself was being held steady. For a moment he
had surrendered to the notion that those were the kalds of
the Four Thousand, continuing their lives in the microminia-
ture cosmos of the jewel, then had come the understanding
that the opal itself was a container. At its heart would be a
core of unique molecules forming a crystal which might be
smaller than a grain of sugar, and it was *there* that the Four
Thousand lay icily dormant, awaiting resurrection on another
world.

He had stared at the ring for many minutes in reverence and
fear before daring to remove it from its carved niche and slip it
on to his finger. The third finger of the left hand had been an
instinctive choice. The platinum band had slid over the joints

158

with ease, but on reaching the base of his finger the metal had stirred for an instant, coiling on his flesh and locking itself in place. There was no undue feeling of pressure, but Jerome knew better than to try removing the ring. He had become truly wedded, entered on a strange contract which was beyond his power to break.

In a way he had surrendered his status as a Terran, and yet did not regard himself as a traitor to his kind. As Conforden had once pointed out, the Dorrinian people were as one with the people of Earth, and it was unthinkable that they should be doomed to slow extinction under the surface of Mercury. There were also many people like Birkett, Thwaite and Starzynski who deserved the chance to return home. Jerome still had reservations about the method chosen for establishing a Dorrinian nation on Earth, but he acknowledged that a *fait accompli* could be the only practicable way.

It was ironic, Jerome thought, that his conscience should give him few qualms on such a vast and contentious issue, while at the same time he felt so guilty over lying to Buxton and Teinert about comparative trivia. They both had a fondness for jokes and wordplay, and were easy to make laugh, especially when they thought he had revealed a comic misunderstanding of all things American. It was something he had used more than once to divert a conversation away from a sensitive area. . . .

"How come," Buxton had said on one early occasion, "we didn't know that Russia had a four-man ship with interplanetary capability?"

"It was a matter of national security. The ZR-12 had many military applications. No country advertises these things."

Buxton had been dissatisfied. "Why was a military ship sent chasing off to Mercury?"

"What else could we have sent? Besides, if the object on Mercury really was the product of an advanced interstellar civilization the knowledge to be gained from it could have been useful in many spheres—including defence."

Buxton had scowled and said, "I thought Krypton was only in the funny papers."

"You have comics about rare gases?"

And at another time Buxton had turned away from the communications panel with an expression which hinted that something had revived his early antagonism towards Jerome.

"That was Allbright calling from the Cape," he had said. "He told me the Soviets have issued a statement denying all knowledge of an interplanetary ship which was sent to Mercury."

"It is an embarrassment," Jerome had replied. "The first reaction is always to deny everything."

"They also deny all knowledge of you."

"How could they acknowledge my presence on Mercury after having disallowed by means of getting there? The statements will change. A story will evolve."

"You know," Teinert had come in, "you speak really good English."

"You are very kind."

"Your accent doesn't even sound Russian to me."

Jerome had produced a rueful smile. "When you come from a place as remote as Okhotsk your *Russian* doesn't even sound Russian."

Once when they were discussing the riddle of the decoy Buxton had said, "Pavel, when you were hanging around waiting for us to show up, did you take a close look at that chunk of metal?"

"Not really," Jerome had said. "I was too worried about dying."

"It looked sort of . . . unused, and it was really *soft*. We were able to saw bits off like it was cardboard. It's hard to imagine a thing like that being part of an operational ship."

"It's all very puzzling."

"You're telling me," Buxton had said gloomily. "What do you think it is?"

"That's outside my field of expertise."

"What is your field of expertise?"

"I'm sorry," Jerome had replied, lost for an answer he would be able to back up in a technical discussion. "I'm not at liberty to divulge that information."

That was a formula he had used time after time when his knowledge of Russian geography, current affairs or space science had proved inadequate to deal with a question. As the journey had progressed and the Soviet news agency had persisted with the absolute denials of Jerome's claims, he had feared that his attitude might cause stresses, but to his relief the two astronauts chose to make a joke of it.

"I'm not at liberty to divulge that information", became a stock reply to queries about sexual attitudes, the time of day or the whereabouts of a pencil.

Other sources of amusement to Buxton and Teinert were Jerome's height and his physical weakness on the exercise machines. When first starting to move around in the Precinct he had judged himself to be a few centimetres taller than in his previous incarnation. In the absence of any comparative measures, and while surrounded by slender Dorrinians, that had seemed a reasonable estimate. It was, however, part of the astronauts' duties to check their own height regularly and chart the increase caused by zero gravity, and they had quickly brought it to Jerome's notice that he was more than two metres tall.

"You must have been out here a hell of a long time, Pavel," Teinert had said. "Did you lose your way?"

Jerome had taken the ribbing with good humour, responding with stories about having been a midget when he began astronaut training, but his lack of strength was a matter for genuine concern to him. His Dorrinian frame was the product of a gravity only four-tenths that of Earth, which meant that its natural weight would be more than doubled when Jerome set foot on his home world. How difficult was it going to be to walk, or even stand up? What about his heart? Would he ever adapt to the higher gravity?

The questions added to the already impenetrable screen which hid the near future. Throughout his life he had always been able to make a reasonable guess at what he would be doing in the following week, and even though events had sometimes proved him wrong it had not happened often enough to destroy the comforting illusion of control, of being able to steer a chosen course. But at this juncture he could see only a matter of hours ahead and the path was quickly lost in a fog of uncertainties.

In addition to all his old misgivings about world reaction to what might be seen as a Dorrinian invasion, he had acquired a new set of worries when he had decided to transport the Thabbren to its destination—and most of them were centred around the menacing figure of Belzor.

Assuming that Belzor had successfully evaded the Dorrinian agents in the Antarctic—and a deep instinct told him that was the case—what would the wayward superman do next? The news stories about the *Quicksilver* having rescued a stranded Russian cosmonaut would not have deceived him for a second. He would have understood at once that the passenger was either a true Dorrinian or a Terran transplant escaping to Earth, and he would certainly have considered the possibility of the Thabbren being on the returning ship. Jerome understood Belzor well enough to know that he would unhesitatingly slay everybody on the *Quicksilver* just as a precaution. It was perhaps surprising that there had been no telepathic attack such as the one which had killed Marmorc, but there were many aspects of telepathy which Jerome did not understand.

In retrospect, having felt the stunning power of a super-telepath's mind, he had realized that the Guardians in the terminal chamber could have prevented his escape without

162

even raising a finger. Chastening though it was to do so, he had to presume that the Guardians had leaped far ahead of him in their thinking and might even have known what he was going to do before the awareness had reached his own consciousness. But there was some comfort in the thought that they must also have analysed Belzor's possible responses and would not have permitted Jerome to take the Thabbren into the ship unless they were confident it would reach Earth in safety. Perhaps—strange thought—it was only super-tele-paths who were vulnerable to psychic attack from an inter-planetary distance. Perhaps Belzor, like a poisonous insect which can sting only once, had sacrificed some vital consti-tuent of his being in that transcendentally lethal onslaught and could not repeat it. Or, to apply plain Terran-style pragmat-ism, it might be that Belzor saw no point in taking a long shot at a target which was winging its way towards him. . . .

"I can see a shuttle," Teinert called from the opposite side of the cabin. "They're coming up to get you, Pavel baby. How does it feel?"

"Great." Jerome shifted his position so that he could see the gleaming wedge-shaped speck which was almost lost in the rolling immensities of Earth. What he could not see was the NASA space station, *Reagan I*, which was slipping along just ahead of the *Quicksilver* in an identical orbit, like a bead on the same invisible wire.

There had been a great deal of high-level activity in the past few days, and as the outcome of unknown numbers of political and military exchanges it had been decided that Jerome's necessary visit to the station should be kept as brief as possible. Buxton and Teinert were scheduled to spend several days there as part of their debriefing programme, but the controversial Russian/non-Russian castaway—the stateless as-tronaut—was to be whisked through in a matter of minutes, presumably for security reasons. The station, though sup-posedly a civilian research establishment, was known to be of strategic importance to the military.

"It looks like you'll soon be home," Hal Buxton said, studiedly casual.

"Yes." Jerome knew him well enough to pick up the faint emphasis on the last word. It was an indirect reference to the fact that the Soviet Union was still categorically denying all knowledge of Jerome. As part of the relationship tacitly agreed upon by the three men, the question of Jerome's origins was no longer discussed. That was the working arrangement, devised to suit the psychological needs of men in a near-impossible situation. He accepted their unprovable tales about marathon drinking and sexual exploits and the landing of giant fish—and they accepted his unprovable claim to have been born in a place more remote from their everyday experience than fabulous Samarkand. But the long journey was ending, and the transient need to believe was being ground away by the obdurate need to know.

"Perhaps you'll send us a picture postcard," Teinert said. "If they have those things in Okhotsk."

Jerome could feel the barriers dropping into place. "Look," he said desperately, "there are times when you have to go against yourself."

Buxton grinned. "I know—and there's information you're not at liberty to divulge."

"I didn't mean it like that."

"I'm sorry," Buxton said with what might have been genuine sincerity. "What do you think is going to happen when you get down there?"

"That's a good question," Jerome replied, his gaze fixed on the silent-climbing shuttle. "A very good question."

164

Chapter 12

"Hello," the Government man said as he manoeuvred himself into the seat beside Jerome. "My name is Dexter Simm, and the first thing I'm going to do is copy your fingerprints. I'm sure you won't mind, but even if you do mind I'm going to copy them anyway, and if necessary I'll get these gentlemen to hold you down while I'm doing it."

Simm inclined his head in the direction of two impassive young men who sat at the front end of the shuttle's passenger compartment. They wore business suits which conspicuously had been chosen to look inconspicuous, and they gave Jerome the impression of being expert at physically subduing people.

"I don't mind," he said lightly, offering Simm both his hands, "but is this the way you greet all Russian visitors?"

"Russian my ass! I don't know where you're from, big man, but you're not Russian."

Working swiftly, Simm pressed Jerome's fingertips against a slip of plastic which he then slid into a flat black box. One of his subordinates left his seat and came down the central aisle, swinging along awkwardly in the absence of gravity. He took the box from Simm, carried it up front and disappeared into the screened-off flight deck. Jerome guessed that a world-wide computer check on his prints would have been completed before the shuttle entered the atmosphere, and he derived perverse satisfaction from the thought. If there was one line of enquiry which was guaranteed to draw a blank it was looking for Dorrinian fingerprints in Terran files.

"Nice ring you've got there." Simm tried to touch the jewel on Jerome's left hand and looked up in amusement and surprise when Jerome snatched his hand back. "What are you so jumpy about?"

"What are you so hostile about?" Jerome countered. "Was it something I said?"

"As a matter of fact, that just about sums it up." Simm stared at Jerome for a moment with open dislike. He was a thick-shouldered man, fiftyish and balding, whose body still looked powerful in spite of the fat which had been layered on it by years of sedentary work. His face was that of the corporate hard man—shrewd but unimaginative, knowledgeable but uncultured.

"I've had the job of studying every statement you've made in the last three months," he said, "and I can tell you I've never seen such a total crock of. . . ." Simm broke off as a bell sounded to announce that the shuttle was casting free of the space station. A second later he gripped the arms of his chair in evident alarm as the craft gave a wallowing lurch and the night-black observation ports along one side of the compartment suddenly blazed with sunlight. Engines sounded intermittently, sending vibrations racing through the wall and ceiling panels. Jerome, having voyaged from beyond the Sun, was unaffected, but Simm's face had developed a greyish pallor and there was the transparent ghost of a moustache on his upper lip.

"And you have the nerve to ask why I'm hostile," he said, apparently deciding to sublimate fear into anger. "Just look at the state of me! I shouldn't be up here in this aluminum bucket, playing spacemen. Do you know we nearly had to set up a special department just to deal with you? Nobody could decide if you were an immigration problem, or an FBI problem, or a military problem, or a NASA problem, or a CIA problem, or a KGB . . . Well, no—the Soviet connection got scrubbed pretty fast. Like I said before, you're no Russian."

"I never claimed to be a true Russian," Jerome said. "The Far East Region isn't. . . ."

"Don't start splitting hairs! I'm not in the mood."

Jerome had been too wrapped up in the bizarre complexities of his own life to have thought previously about how various US agencies would react to his claims and his actual arrival on Earth. The one thing he could predict about the near future was that Dorrinian super-telepaths would get to him, no matter where he was, but what was going to become of him after he had handed over the Thabbren? Would the Dorrinians free him from detention, or would he be left to fend off inquisitors until that unimaginable moment when the Great Secret ceased to be a secret?

"If everybody is so convinced that I'm some kind of impostor," he said, buying time in which to think, "why was the *Quicksilver* allowed to bring me back to Earth?"

"Because you're going to be a real mine of information, big man. You don't seem to think so, but you are going to blab everything about how you got to Mercury. The complete works. You're going to name the country that put you there, and you're going to. . . ." Simm paused, apparently beginning to feel more at ease, and for a moment looked out at the phosphorescent whiteness of the space station which was now moving above and ahead of the falling shuttle. "Besides, it wouldn't have been neighbourly to leave you out there— especially after Chuck Baumanis was considerate enough to make room on the ship."

There it is again, Jerome thought. *Instinct rushes in where logic fears to tread. It's part of our nature to look for connections. We need them. . . .*

"I'm sorry about Baumanis," he said. "I don't suppose it's much consolation to you that his death made it possible for another man to live."

"Not much." Simm ran a gloomily critical eye over Jerome. "You know, you're a real mess. Are those the only clothes you've got? Apart from the Mickey Mouse space suit, that is."

Jerome, who had lost the habit of thinking about standards of dress, abruptly realized that he had to be a strange spectacle

167

to Terran eyes. His Dorrinian-made shirt and slacks were in a sack along with the cumbersome vacuum suit in which he had made his break from the tunnel. Aboard the *Quicksilver* he had been provided with disposable plastex coveralls which he had been forced to sever at the waist to accommodate his elongated frame, and the resultant two-piece garment—coupled with the grey socks which were his only footwear—was anything but elegant.

"I see what you mean," he said, "but I guess I'm all right for Florida in January."

"We're not going into the Cape."

"Why not?"

"Too much media interest in you. Too many people milling around. We don't want that, so we're going to an Air Force base in North Dakota."

"I see." Jerome considered the new information, wondering if the arrangement would make it difficult for the Dorrinians to contact him. "You might have picked a warmer spot."

Simm was maliciously amused. "I thought you Russians were used to the cold."

Jerome turned away from him, resolving to say as little as possible during the rest of the descent. Much sooner than he had anticipated the shuttle dipped into the upper levels of the atmosphere and the circles of sky he could see in the ports began to turn blue. Within the space of ten minutes the rush of air over the pressure skin and control surfaces had become audible and the shuttle, exchanging the characteristics of a ballistic missile for those of an aircraft, began to hint at having a mechanical personality of its own, expressed in occasional yaws and tilts and flirts of its tail.

As far as Jerome could determine from his fragmentary glimpses, much of central Canada and the USA was under cloud cover. The prospect of a buffeting descent through bad weather prompted him to tighten his safety harness, and it was while working with the connectors that he realized his arms were laden with invisible weight. He had allowed the problems of Earth's gravity to drift out of his thoughts, hoping he had been unduly pessimistic about his ability to compensate, but this was an unpleasant foretaste of things to come.

Aware that his neck muscles were protesting about the extra strain, Jerome inclined his head forward and was shocked when his chin came down on his collar-bone with a tooth-clicking impact. He brought his head upright with an effort, feeling as though it were encased in a lead helmet, and found that Simm was looking at him in obvious concern.

"Say, are you all right?" Simm said, his gaze darting over Jerome's face. "Do you need a medic?"

"Too long in zero gravity," Jerome told him, trying to come to terms with the discovery that three months of weightlessness had seriously weakened his already inadequate Dorrinian musculature. "I'm not even sure I'll be able to walk."

"Just so long as you can talk." Simm turned back to his study of the sculptured cloudscapes into which the shuttle was plunging.

Jerome swore silently at him and concentrated on keeping his neck straight and his head upright as the observation ports abruptly greyed out and the descent became rough. All the sensations of motion were enhanced by his weakness, and for him the flight became a continuous sequence of falls, twists and shimmies which made him feel that the unseen pilot was barely winning the battle for control. The reality of the return to his home world was at a far remove from the nostalgic visions which had made the long nights in the Precinct seem endless. Threatened by elemental dangers, feeble as an invalid, he was being thrust into a dark arena in whose shadows hid a malign and terrifying superman who wanted him dead. Belzor was a being who unhesitatingly killed those who obstructed the most minor of his interests—and as long as Jerome carried the Thabbren he embodied the threat of death itself to Belzor . . .

Feeling isolated and vulnerable, Jerome cupped his right hand over the opal ring and clenched it in a double fist as the

169

shuttle dropped below the cloud ceiling. There were glimpses of barren snowfields stretching away into greyness, of thinly etched roads running sparsely from nowhere to nowhere. Earth was not in a welcoming mood. Turbines at the rear of the shuttle were spun into life for the final part of the flight and made a new contribution to the forces acting on Jerome's body, drawing his head back each time they surged. Minutes later there was a blurring rush of lights outside, a lingering moment of near-silence and the shuttle clumped solidly on to concrete. Jerome sat still, gazing straight in front during a thunderous landing run, and only when the shuttle had come to a halt did he turn the precariously balanced weight of his head to look at Simm.

"Now that that's over," he said. "I demand to be taken to the Soviet Embassy in Washington."

"Sure, sure," Simm replied jovially, rising to his feet and clicking his fingers at the two watchful young men. "One of you guys is going to have to do without his overcoat here—we can't risk our visitor catching cold."

Interested in testing the extent of his disability, Jerome unfastened his harness and forced himself into a standing position. He was relieved to find that he could in fact stand alone, albeit with some circling of his knees, which showed there had been a real benefit from the exercise machine in the *Quicksilver*. It was unfortunate that he had not thought of trying to strengthen his neck, but at least he was going to be spared the indignity of having to be carried off the shuttle. Feeling as though he had been burdened with more than his own weight of sandbags, he advanced along the central aisle to the front of the compartment on quivering legs, with Simm following close behind.

One of Simm's men, looking distinctly unhappy, helped him into a tweed overcoat he had taken from a locker. While he was buttoning the coat he became aware of uniformed flight crew at work in the airlock section which lay immediately forward of the passenger compartment. A few seconds later there was the *thunk* of a massive door settling into its open position and tendrils of chilly air invaded the warmth of the ship.

"Let's go, big man." Simm squeezed past Jerome and preceded him down a metal stair which someone on the ground had wheeled into place beside the shuttle's fuselage. Jerome glanced wordlessly around the group who were waiting for him to leave, then ventured uncertainly on to the stair. The afternoon sky was a leaden grey, much darker than the snow covered ground, and only a few specks of amber lights close to the horizon indicated the existence of airfield buildings. The shuttle had come to rest in a lonely avenue of runway marker beacons, and was surrounded by an entourage made up of fire tenders, rescue vehicles and two dark-windowed black limousines.

Jerome had barely taken in the scene when the cold closed in on him like an assassin pouncing from ambush. He gasped with shock, unable to recall such savagery in even the hardest winter, then came the realization that physically he had never experienced *any* real coldness. As well as being pitiably frail, his inherited Dorrinian body was adapted to the unvarying warmth of Cuthtranel. Already shivering violently, Jerome groped his way down the stair and almost cried aloud when his stockinged feet touched the thin coating of snow on the runway. The crews of the encircling vehicles had remained in their cabs, probably under orders, but Jerome knew they were watching him and some remnant of pride forced him to stand upright and conceal his distress.

This is going to kill me, he thought. *Belzor doesn't need to get involved.*

"Okay, here's what we do," Simm said, addressing the two agents who had descended the stair behind Jerome. "I'll go with my new pal here in my car, and you follow us to the Boeing in the second. Stay on the ground and keep everything under surveillance while we're getting ready for take-off, then join us on board. And for God's sake don't look so miserable,

171

Dougan." He paused to slap the coatless agent on the shoulder. "I'll see to it that you get your Abercombie and Fitch back in good shape. Okay? Now let's go!"

Simm grabbed Jerome by the upper arm and urged him towards the nearer of the two limousines. Jerome was resentful of the casual manhandling, but was totally unable to offer any resistance. Chilled and barely able to stand, he was swept along by Simm's bulk as though he had been caught up in some irresistible machine. As they reached the limousine someone inside opened a rear door, facilitating Simm in the task of guiding Jerome's helpless body into the back seat. Simm came in after him, closed the door and sat opposite on an aft-facing fold-down.

The limousine moved off immediately, its driver invisible behind a smoked glass partition. Simm's companion, who had moved on to the other fold-down, was a lean, blade-nosed man of about forty, dressed in the bland suiting of his trade. He was staring solemnly at Jerome's left hand. After a few seconds he slid down on to his knees and Simm did likewise, also gazing at the opal ring, his face rapt. A new uneasiness penetrated Jerome's physical discomfort.

"Rayner Jerome," Simm said, "we honour you as the Bearer of the Thabbren."

His companion nodded. "We honour you."

"I. . . ." Jerome exhaled shakily. "I ought to know what's going on here . . . but it's all so. . . ."

"You've been through a long ordeal and naturally you're confused," Simm said. "I didn't help matters with the way I treated you on the shuttle, but I had to put on a good show for the benefit of Dougan and McAllister and the crew. They are all Terrans."

Jerome had to utter the redundant words. "But you're a Dorrinian."

"Yes," Simm said. "I am a Guardian, as is Peter Voegle here, and Cy Rickell, who is driving the car. We will continue to use our Terran names for the present. The last-minute switching of your landing from the Cape caused some difficulties, but we still have the situation under control."

"That's true, but we have to act quickly now," Voegle added, beginning to remove his jacket. "I'm going to put on your clothes, Rayner. Then I will go on the plane to Washington with Dexter in your place."

Floundering, still numb with the cold, Jerome could only assimilate one new idea at a time. "You're going to pretend to be me?"

"That's correct."

"But if Dougan and McWhatever are Terrans . . . I mean, they'll remember my face."

"No, they won't," Simm said, almost smiling. "They'll remember what we want them to remember. All the others who saw you will be outside our control, of course, so we won't be able to maintain the deception for more than a day or two—but that should be long enough. Now, let me help you out of that overcoat."

"Hold on," Jerome pleaded. "What about me? What's going to happen to me?"

"We've brought a complete set of clothing which should fit someone your height. Cy Rickell will drive you to a private airfield near Grand Forks. It's only about an hour from here. An aircraft belonging to CryoCare will be waiting to fly you to Amity. It will have to follow an overland route the whole way down the two American continents, because we can't risk an accident in which the plane comes down at sea, but the journey won't take more than. . . ."

"Stop!" Desperation prompted Jerome to raise his left hand, knuckles outwards, borrowing the talismanic power of the jewel. "I've gone far enough . . . *done* enough . . . I'm not going to the Antarctic. Somebody else can take the ring—I'm finished with the bloody thing."

"Please don't speak that way, Rayner." Simm glanced unhappily at Voegle, who had frozen in the act of peeling off his shirt. "Don't speak about the Thabbren in that way."

173

"I'm sorry," Jerome replied. "But I meant what I said. Somebody else has to take it."

"But you are the *Bearer* of the Thabbren. It has accepted you and now you are a direct instrument of the Four Thousand. Have you ever tried taking the ring off?"

"No." It suddenly struck Jerome as odd that he had never removed the jewel from his finger.

"Try it now."

"Fine!" Jerome calmly gripped the opal ring between his right thumb and forefinger, and then—just as calmly—let go of it and allowed his hand to fall to his side. There had been no neural shock, no telepathic thunder, but he understood that the ring had to stay on his finger. It was something he knew with the clean, uncomplicated certainty of a small child—the ring had to stay on his finger.

"This isn't fair," he said. "Why do you people have to work this way? If you want me to take the Thabbren down to Amity, why don't you blank me out and make me a zombie, or make me think I'm going somewhere on vacation? Why do I have to go *scared*?"

"We are a very ethical people," Simm said, his voice persuasively gentle. "We don't want to rob you of your free will or turn you into a biological machine. It would be much more in keeping with our ethic if you made a free choice to do what is right."

"That's beautiful," Jerome said bitterly. "While you sit back and congratulate yourself on your wonderful ethics, I have to go up against Belzor."

"*Belzor!*" Simm exclaimed, his expression a blend of surprise and pleasure. "I'm so sorry, Rayner. It was criminal of me not to have told you at the start, but we have all been under a lot of pressure."

Jerome looked from one man to the other. "What about Belzor?"

"He's dead," Simm said peacefully. "The Prince is dead."

Chapter 13

Jerome slept during most of the flight to the Antarctic, but—although he was no longer afraid for his life—his sleep was troubled by strangely pessimistic dreams.

He had listened to accounts of how a team of some twenty Dorrinians, forsaking their code of non-violence, had armed themselves and hunted down Prince Belzor. They had found him in a well-equipped bivouac near the southern tip of the Amity condominium. Although three days had passed since the death of Marmorc on Mercury, the Prince had still been in a state approaching catalepsy, so drained of vital energies that he had been unable to move or put up any kind of telepathic defence. A Dorrinian had promptly injected air into Belzor's blood-stream, producing a complete cessation of the already feeble heart activity within thirty seconds. The body, apparently dead from natural causes, had then been placed in a snowdrift more than a kilometre from the tent. Although it had been the beginning of Spring in the Antarctic, there had been a blizzard in progress in that part of Graham Land and the temperature had been -18°C. The body had quickly been lost to view under a layer of powdery snow, and the Dorrinian execution squad had returned to the CryoCare headquarters and had been dispersed.

"We were very lucky," Paul Nordenskjöld had said to Jerome. "Not one man was lost in the operation—but things would have been very different if the Prince had been in possession of his faculties."

Nordenskjöld, spokesman for the dozen men and women who were also on the flight south, had maintained a discreet distance most of the time, allowing Jerome to rest and adjust to the new circumstances. The news of Belzor's death had brought him a pang of relief—only then could he admit to himself that he had fully expected to die at the hands of the alien superman—but there had been no consequent happiness or peace of mind. The erasure of his fears about Belzor had opened the floodgate for all his pent-up apprehensions about the immediate and long-term future.

The lenticular opal on his finger was an aesthetically pleasing object; the story of the Dorrinian people and their dream was one of epic grandeur and courage; the word "reincarnation" was charged with ethereal and spiritual connotations— but underlying all the lofty abstractions were realities of a different order. Realities such as four thousand diseased corpses. Jerome was on his way to a strange rendezvous with those corpses, bringing them the gift of life. But what sort of life was it going to be? The Dorrinians believed their infant statelet would quickly win acceptance among the nations of Earth, but Jerome could see nuclear augmentations of the *aurora australis*. In a world where mutilation and death were common penalties for incorrect skin pigmentation, what were the prospects for an alien sept whose origins reeked of every death taboo known to mankind?

Furthermore, what were his personal prospects? What was the outlook for a spindly giant, crushed by a body weight two-and-a-half times its norm, willing conscript of the undead, traitor to every man, woman and child on Earth?

How can all this have happened to me? Jerome had asked himself the question more than once during the flight. *A major calamity should be the outcome of a major mistake, but all I did was stop off at an ordinary suburban house in Whiteford on my way to work.*

If only I had driven on by. . . .

"We'll be landing in about ten minutes," Nordenskjöld said, rousing Jerome from his uneasy drowsing. He was a swarthy man whose tight-curled black hair and Italianate features were ill-matched with his Nordic name. His bur-

176

gundy necktie, like those of the other men, bore the CC symbol of CryoCare.

"Thank you." Jerome levered himself upright with difficulty and glanced at the time display on the walnut panelling of the executive suite he was occupying. It said 14.08.

"We have dropped about twenty minutes behind schedule because we were forced to make a wide detour around Santiago," Nordenskjöld explained. "The city was hit by a tactical nuclear weapon two days ago, and the Chileans are firing at everything they see."

"It's so good to be back." Jerome looked at the quilted snowsuit which Nordenskjöld was offering him and thought about having to venture into the polar coldness. "Before you cram me into that thing, may I try the brandy again?"

"Of course." Nordenskjöld went to a cocktail cabinet and returned with a glass of brandy. Jerome, who had rarely drunk alcohol in his old incarnation, had impulsively ordered brandy earlier in the flight. He had been hoping to find some hint of comfort in the warmth of the drink, but his Dorrinian senses had revolted at the taste. This time the reaction was less severe and he was able to get three sips down before his stomach gave a tentative heave. He handed the glass back, grateful for the glow which was kindling inside him, and struggled into the duvet garment with Nordenskjöld's aid.

"Hey, am I going on some kind of expedition?" he said as another man brought him thick-soled thermal boots.

"You will only have to walk a short distance from a personnel transporter to the entrance of the Cryodome, but the temperature is in the region of minus thirty at the moment," Nordenskjöld said. "And it's almost as cold inside the dome."

"I see," Jerome said, filled with a sudden desperate yearning to have done with everything that was cold and inhuman, alien and unnatural. "Exactly what is going to happen when I go in there? Will I have to look at thousands of dead bodies?"

"I can't discuss these things with you."

"But I'm the Bearer of the Thabbren."

"You're not a Guardian."

"Well, whatever's going to happen, I hope it's over soon. I just want to get it over with." As though triggered by Jerome's words, the seat belt warning signs began to glow. A faint rumbling sound accompanied by a momentary tilting sensation told him the aircraft had spread its metal plumage to the full for a landing. He looked out of the nearest window and experienced a *deja vu* sensation as he saw a scene almost identical to his first glimpse of North Dakota. The entire world seemed to be made of trackless snowfields, frozen in perpetual twilight. A minute later the aircraft touched down on a strip of heated mesh and gradually came to a halt with a roar of reverse thrusting engines. Nordenskjöld and the others remained immobile in their seats until the turbines had given their last dying wail and the warning lights were extinguished.

No point in rushing things at the last minute, Jerome thought. *Not after a wait of three-and-a-half thousand years.*

He tried to imagine what was going through the Dorrinians' minds as they moved stolidly and silently about the aircraft, adjusting snowsuits and gloves, collecting belongings from lockers, behaving much like commuters at the end of a routine flight. The task was impossible, he realized. Only a devout Christian who had actually observed the Second Coming could have an inkling of what these minutes meant to these ordinary looking men and women who had made the awesome mental leap between worlds in the furtherance of a dream.

Jerome felt compelled to be silent as the passenger exit was opened and stairs were put in place from below. He stood up and found that the hours of rest during the flight had made little difference to his physical incapacity. His head rolled grotesquely and his knees tended to buckle with every plodding step, as though he had been weighted down with many sandbags. He was breathing heavily by the time he got out on to the small platform at the head of the stair.

"I don't want to be carried," he said to Nordenskjöld as several men steadied him with solicitous hands.

"I quite understand." Nordenskjöld nodded gravely. "It would also be better for us if the Bearer of the Thabbren arrived with dignity."

"So be it." Holding his breath to lessen the pain the gelid air was inflicting on his nostrils, Jerome fixed his eyes on the nearest of the track-laying vehicles which were waiting beside the plane and made his way to it. He tried to step up into its passenger compartment unaided, but his legs were simply unable to raise his body the short distance against the implacable pull of the planet. Others, seemingly gifted with Herculean power, half-lifted him and guided him into a seat. Only Nordenskjöld joined him in the compartment. There was a moment's delay while the rest of the party boarded the other vehicles, then the little convoy moved off in the direction of distant blue-white lights.

Here we go, Jerome thought. *One last little chore to perform for these people, and then I . . . That's the question. Take up permanent residence in a wheelchair? In a hydrotherapy unit?*

The surrounding bleakness served to depress his mood even further, and insulated in his cocoon of introspection he scarcely noticed when the vehicle began passing through gateways in wire fences. It was only when it crawled to a halt at a flat dome of a building, more than a hundred metres across, that he was again touched by the unearthly mystery and power of the occasion. His heart began a steady drumbeat as he realized that the unique moment was at hand, the moment when the histories of two worlds would fuse into one—with incalculable results.

The Four Thousand were about to be roused from their millennia-long slumber.

"We can go no closer to the entrance," Nordenskjöld said, interrupting his reverie. "Do you think you can walk that far?"

Jerome studied the fan-shaped flight of steps which rose to the dome's entrance. They were very wide, curving to the line of the building's perimeter, and very shallow, gently ascending between granite windbreaks and heaps of cleared snow. This was where the Dorrinian he had seen die on the surface of Mercury should have walked in majesty and triumph as the chosen Bearer of the Thabbren, but fate had decreed that Rayner Jerome should take his place.

"I'll be all right," Jerome said. "Just put me on my feet."

He waited without moving, not daring to negotiate the drop to the ground on his own, until Nordenskjöld had descended. The Dorrinian helped him out of the vehicle and stood back, looking pale and tense, as Jerome swayed for a second and then began his laboured ascent to the dome's dark-shadowed entrance. Jerome reached the first step, raised his right foot on to it with comparative ease, and by leaning forward and exerting all the strength of his thigh successfully elevated the rest of his body. His left foot trailed into place beside the other, and he was stable again.

That wasn't too bad, he thought. *Only seven more to go.*

Two unexpected events occurred simultaneously.

Behind Jerome, Paul Nordenskjöld emitted a tortured cry.

And ahead of Jerome, to the right of the stair, a mound of snow broke open, powdering away in the breeze, to disclose the figure of a man who was carrying a rifle.

Jerome, transfixed by fright, gaped at the apparition. The man raised his free hand and slowly drew back the hood of his parka, giving Jerome a clear view of his face, a face which had a strange familiarity to it. Jerome gave a quavering sigh as recognition came to him.

There was a moment of tumultuous silence, then the man said, "That's right, Rayner—against all the odds, we meet again."

Had Jerome been able he would have fled, obeying the dictates of instinct, heedless of his inability to outpace a bullet, but he was in the grip of a sick paralysis and all he could do was stand, teetering, on the first step and stare at the face which had once been his own.

180

They lied to me, he thought numbly. *They lied because they knew I could never face this.*

"No, they didn't lie," Belzor said. "The fools had me—they actually *had* me!—and it's a measure of their sheer incompetence that I'm still alive."

Jerome willed his legs to let him back away, but all that happened was that a shudder went through his body.

Belzor gave a barely perceptible shake of his head. "You can't leave, Rayner—not until you know all that you ought to know, all that your friends have kept from you."

"You're supposed to be dead," Jerome mumbled.

"Yes, I made a serious mistake when I disposed of Marmorc the way I did," Belzor said. "Under normal circumstances twenty Dorrinians would have been no match for me, not even when they had overcome their naïve prejudice against your world's beautiful weaponry, but I was too weak to fight them. The only way I could win the struggle was by making them believe I had lost it—and that was *so* easy to do. The intelligent course would have been for them to fire bullets through my brain, but the fools weren't even aware that I was influencing them when they contented themselves with stopping my heart and leaving me to freeze."

Belzor smiled calmly. "This body I inherited from you was in extremely bad condition, Rayner. You would have died from arteriosclerosis within a matter of months, but now it is perfect and will continue to be that way for many years."

Jerome, distraught and faint, became aware that another voice—a telepathic voice—was sounding above the clamour of his thoughts. *The Prince cannot harm you, Rayner. He made a mistake in coming here. He has not regained his former powers, and we are containing him. He is unable to move or aim the rifle at you. Take the Thabbren into the dome.*

"The fools are right in one respect," Belzor said. "My kald energy has been greatly depleted, and for that reason they are able to contain me. It is an even match at present—tens

181

of Guardians against one of me—but they are wrong to believe that I have made a mistake in meeting you here."

The power of hatred enabled Jerome to speak firmly. "It *was* a mistake, Belzor. You tried to kill me."

Belzor smiled again, unperturbed. "I fired at you and missed. You fired at me and hit. That more than put you even."

"It wasn't a game—you killed Pitman."

"You're not seriously concerned about that, are you? A Dorrinian body-snatcher! An alien invader who was in the very act of setting you up for a transfer! Be logical, Rayner."

"I'm trying to be logical," Jerome said, emboldened by the assurance that Belzor posed no physical threat. "And I still say you made a mistake in coming here."

"But consider my alternative. I could have gone into hiding somewhere and allowed you to deliver the Thabbren, to reincarnate four thousand powerful Dorrinians who have good reason to want me dead. That would have been the real mistake."

The Prince cannot prevent you delivering the Thabbren, a silent voice told Jerome. *Carry it into the dome now!*

Jerome took a pace towards the next stair. "You tried to kill me, Belzor."

"I underestimated you that day at the lake, Rayner," Belzor said. "The fact that you are back on this planet shows how much I underestimated you, but that is part of the past. I now know that you are intelligent enough to do what is best for you and your own people. That is my justification for meeting you here—I am staking my life on your intelligence."

"But. . . ." Jerome stiffened his legs to steady the leaden weight of his body. "I don't know what you mean."

"I mean that you are going to give *me* the Thabbren. You, of your own free will, are going to give *me* the Thabbren and allow *me* to draw off its kald energies, thus consigning the Four Thousand to oblivion, for ever."

Carry the Thabbren into the dome NOW!

182

Jerome raised weighted arms and pressed his hands to his temples. "Why?" he said to Belzor. "Why should I do as you say?"

"Because, Rayner, I am going to tell you the truth about the Four Thousand . . . the truth which has been so carefully concealed from you by your highly ethical friends . . . and when you hear it. . . ."

There was a screaming and a keening in Jerome's mind, echoes of telepathic warfare rolling and reverberating through neural pathways. He saw Belzor stagger and grow pale.

"And when you hear it," Belzor ground out, each word like the splintering of a bone, "you will decide, of your own free will, that the Four Thousand have no place in your world . . . or in any other. . . ."

CARRY THE THABBREN INTO THE DOME NOW!

"The Guardians grow angry and afraid, but they can't impose their will on you while I am alive. Listen to me and make your own decision, Rayner Jerome." Belzor paused, looking as though he might fall, and when he spoke again his voice seemed weaker. "The Four Thousand, whose kalds you brought to Earth, were absolute controllers of Dorrin before the Days of the Comet. They were super-telepaths who had interlinked to form a composite mind of almost infinite power. You have seen what a single super-telepath can do. Try to imagine that ability raised to the power of four thousand.

"If the Dorrinian composite mind is brought into existence again it will be absolute overlord of every being on this planet. It will decide everything. It will *control* everything. As a human being you treasure your free will, Rayner Jerome— and I am telling you now that this could be your last opportunity to make use of it.

"Do not make the wrong decision!"

Jerome found that he was swaying, almost losing the battle to keep his burdensome body upright. He was breathing hard, and the cold was tearing at his lungs, but the pain was remote and unimportant. The coppery disc of the Sun, almost quenched in the greyness of the horizon, was dimly illuminating a battlefield. There was no sound from the Dorrinians behind him, and Belzor had fallen silent—watching and waiting—but there was a psychic conflict raging all about him, even though he could barely sense its shivers and shocks. And he, trapped at the centre of the battle, was being required to make an impossible decision, without even being sure that Belzor's fantastic assertion was true.

"I speak the truth," Belzor said. "Look at me."

Jerome looked at the face which had once been his own, saw the eyes begin to lase, felt the beginnings of the special pain. . . .

And he was on Earth twenty thousand years earlier, vicariously present as the colonists from space set up their encampments and spread their civilization, untroubled by competition from the indigenous tribes. The settlers were not surprised to find human beings already present—most of the suitable worlds in that region of space had been seeded during long-forgotten migrations—and they were on a technological crest which made them confident of their ability to deal with any adversity.

But the first major threat came from within.

A successful mutation occurred, creating individuals who possessed certain psi powers, including that of telepathy. The dominant genes of the mutation would have permeated the entire gene pool in the normal course of events, but the non-psi majority quickly became alarmed and took action to isolate the mutants. They chose to place them on the planet nearest the Sun because its natural conditions would force the mutants to live underground, unable to develop the physical resources needed for space travel.

But they failed to foresee that the telepaths would breed super-telepaths, and that the super-telepaths would coalesce into composite entities of increasing size and power, reaching the ultimate in the form of the Four Thousand—the vast aggregate mind which assumed total control of every aspect of life on the planet. . . .

The pain faded and Jerome saw that Belzor had sunk to his knees. The near-subliminal shrilling in Jerome's mind was rising in pitch and intensity, becoming unbearable, evidence that the psi battle was nearing its climax.

"It's time for you to make that decision, Rayner," Paul Nordenskjöld said from behind Jerome. "We are slowly overcoming the Prince, and in an hour's time we will be able to take the decision out of your hands. But for the present you retain your freedom of choice. Are you going to use it wisely? Are you going to side with the evil that is Belzor, allow him to destroy the Thabbren, and accept whatever reward he decides to give you?"

"I'll make you immortal," Belzor whispered. "I'll give you body after body. You can live for ever."

Nordenskjöld responded at once. "Think carefully, Rayner. You know what Belzor is. As soon as he has the Thabbren in his hands he will kill every Dorrinian here, and quite probably he will kill you as well. But even if he did keep his promise there would be no eternal life for you—because your world is rushing to destruction. The coming nuclear winter will see the end of all human life on this planet.

"And that brings us to the other choice you can make on behalf of every man, woman and child on Earth.

"All you have to do is carry the Thabbren into the dome, and there will be an end to war. And to famine. And to disease. And to crime against man, and crime against the planet. Your cherished free will can never have been as precious to you as at this moment, Rayner. We don't offer eternal life to you as a person—but your kind can grow as old as the Sun."

Jerome stood quite still for three beats of his jolting heart, then he began to walk towards the dark entrance of the dome. His knees sagged at every step and he knew that if he fell it would be impossible for him to rise again, but he managed to move in a straight line and to prevent his head from wobbling. It was important that the Bearer of the Thabbren should arrive with dignity.

185

Belzor's voice was tortured, so faint that it might have been a telepathic communication. "Don't be a *fool*, Jerome! Don't let them trick you! Do you really believe you're acting under your own free will at this moment? Do you think you have *ever* had. . . ?"

Jerome continued walking towards the dome.

The circular main chamber was filled with a chill white mist which all but obscured the banks of metred caskets. Rows of ceiling lights glowed like faint greenish moons. At a central location on the floor was a slim pedestal which terminated in a large hemispherical crystal. Jerome knew without being told, as in a dream, that he must go to the pedestal. He was no longer aware of the physical process of walking.

As in a dream, he approached the pedestal and saw there was a disc of platinum set into the crystal's flat upper surface. As in a dream, he removed his left glove.

The opal ring of the Thabbren slid off his finger easily, and he placed it on the disc.

There was no sound, no visible consequence of his action, but the etheric agitation in his mind, the nearly-heard clamour of telepathic conflict, came to an abrupt end.

Belzor is dead, he thought, without emotion. He turned away from the pedestal, intending to walk back to the group who were waiting at the chamber's entrance, but the weight of his body was suddenly insupportable, the fierce gravity of Earth too much to contend with any longer. He stumbled and went down hard on to his knees, and waited helplessly while Nordenskjöld and another man rushed to his aid. They raised him to his feet and carried him out of the chamber and its shifting silvered mists into an anteroom.

Jerome tried to smile at Nordenskjöld as he was being placed in a chair. "I didn't expect to be so . . . so *weak*. I don't know if I can go on like this for very long."

"You won't have to," Nordenskjöld said. "We reward our own."

"But I don't see what you can. . . ."

There was an instant of pain, the special pain, and Jerome found himself kneeling in the drifted snow beside the flight of steps leading up to the Cryodome. He stood up and, even in his turmoil of shock and confusion, was aware that the action had been accomplished with complete lack of effort. There was a solid object in his right hand. He looked down at the rifle and—trying to express the inexpressible—threw the weapon away, sending it whirling high over the windbreaks.

His body and soul had been reunited, and he felt *right*. There was nothing in the universe, he realized, which could have compensated for the loss of that feeling. He turned and walked towards the dome, noting that his unaided vision was now perfect. He was on the top step when Nordenskjöld emerged from the dark rectangle of the entrance.

"You don't have to spend any more time here, Rayner," Nordenskjöld said as he took Jerome's arm and turned him away from the circular building. "The plane is at your disposal, and you can leave as soon as it is refuelled."

"Wait!" Jerome refused to move. "You can't just drop me like this."

Nordenskjöld's face was solemn. "You have been used and to some extent abused, but you are also being rewarded. Belzor was not lying about your previous life expectancy, but the physical form you now inhabit is as perfect as a human body can. . . ."

"That's not what I meant," Jerome cut in. "What's going to happen about . . . *everything*? Have the Four Thousand been reincarnated? Are they going to contact the United Nations? And what about the. . . .?"

"Not so fast," Nordenskjöld said, beginning to smile. "We are not going to rush things—not after being patient for thousands of years. The presence of the Four Thousand on Earth will remain secret until the time is ripe. They can work better that way, with less upheaval in your world's affairs. I'm sure you can see that is the best way."

Jerome was dissatisfied. "But what about all the people on Mercury? I was told there was going to be a big space programme to bring them all here."

"That will all be taken care of in due course. The world will be told that the astronaut who was rescued from Mercury died of cardiac arrest, and that he claimed to have been born on Mercury in an underground colony. The Dorrinian vacuum suit and its radio will also be shown in the right places. Those measures will stimulate enough world interest to ensure that there will be more missions to Mercury, and from that point on the situation can develop at its own pace."

"It isn't going to work," Jerome said. "Even if the Dorrinians can keep quiet about the Four Thousand and how they got here, any Terrans you bring back will shout their heads off."

Nordenskjöld shook his head. "No, Rayner. They will say only what the Four Thousand want them to say. They will remember only what the Four Thousand want them to remember."

"Can the Four Thousand exercise that much control over so many people at once?"

"Of course." Nordenskjöld's eyes were locked hard with Jerome's. "That is a simple task."

"What this all boils down to," Jerome said steadily, accepting that it would be futile to run, "is that something has to be done about me."

"Don't be alarmed, Rayner," Nordenskjöld said with great gentleness. "We are a very ethical people."

Epilogue

It was a fine day in Whiteford, and the whole town was ablaze with sunlit familiarity, glowing with that aura of humdrum comfort, security and sanity which is special to small communities on summer mornings.

Jerome walked to the window of his office and stood for a moment, contentedly looking down through the trees at the activity in Mayflower Square. It was sinfully early to be considering taking the rest of the day off, but in the few months that had elapsed since he had married Anne Kruger and assumed joint editorship of the *Examiner* the workload had become extremely light. The major world stories—such as the dramatically sudden achievement of nuclear disarmament —were not the *Examiner*'s province, and even local crime had all but ceased to exist.

"Are you thinking what I'm thinking?" Anne slipped her arms around him from behind and pressed her face against the hard muscles of his back.

"Yes, but we were at the lake on Tuesday," he said. "We really ought to try working a full week *some* time."

Anne laughed. "Remind me to get you a box of anti-Puritan pills. I'll go in and have a word with Bernard—I'm sure he won't mind taking over." She broke free of Jerome and left the office in search of the deputy editor.

Jerome returned to his desk to wait for her, and on an idle impulse opened one of the drawers and removed a thick file. Its cover bore the single word: QUICKSILVER. The *Examiner*'s readership tended to be more interested in local flower show results than in space flight, but he had made a personal collection of cuttings relating to the *Quicksilver* mission and its sensational return to Earth.

He vividly remembered his sense of disbelief when, back in late January, it had been disclosed that the rescued cosmonaut had claimed to be a member of a human colony which had been established on Mercury in prehistoric times. The mysterious spaceman had died of heart failure soon after his arrival on Earth, but apparently there had been time for him to convince some people that his story was true. World interest had been so intense that three major members of the space club—the USA included—were currently preparing new expeditions to the first planet.

Jerome opened the folder and flicked through it until he reached a photograph of the dead astronaut. He had studied the dark-bearded Christ-like face many times, wondering why it continued to fascinate him. He was quite certain in his own mind it was that of a Russian who had come so close to death on Mercury that he had been driven mad by the ordeal, but did some unacknowledged part of him want to believe otherwise?

"Right, I've fixed it with Bernard," Anne said as she came back into the office. "We can play hookey for the rest of the day."

Jerome looked up at her and smiled. "I'll buy you a soda for that."

"You're at that picture again!" Anne came to his side and looked down at the photograph. "I think you're starting to believe he really did come from Mercury."

"Don't be childish, Anne," Jerome sighed. "I mean, is it *likely*?"

"Then why do you keep looking at his picture?" She nudged his shoulder playfully with her hip. "I'm beginning to think I've got a rival."

"Never." Jerome closed the *Quicksilver* file and dropped it into his waste bin with a flourish which was meant to indicate finality. "I know when I'm well off."

190